STICKY FINGERS

STICKY FINGERS

A TESS CAMILLO MYSTERY

MORGAN HUNT

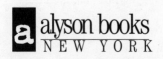
alyson books
NEW YORK

Manufactured in the United States of America.

This trade paperback original is published by Alyson Books,
245 West 17th Street, New York, New York, 10011, Suite 1200.
Distribution in the United Kingdom by Turnaround Publisher Services Ltd.,
Unit 3, Olympia Trading Estate, Coburg Road, Wood Green,
London N22 6TZ England.

First edition: May 2007

07 08 09 10 [a] 10 9 8 7 6 5 4 3 2 1

ISBN 1-59350-003-3
ISBN-13 978-1-59350-003-0

Library of Congress Cataloging-in-Publication Data
is on file.

Designed by Heather Hutchison.

This book is dedicated to:
Dr. Gerald Schneider and Dr. Michele Carpenter
for outstanding surgical skill and care;

Kathleen Daniels and Susan Heath, nurses who
personify knowledgeable compassion;

Dr. J. Min Fan, whose way with herbs, with God's
help, conquered cancer; and

The loved ones who help me celebrate my rescued
life, especially Fran, Maggie, M.J., Robin, Karen,
Glenna, Marion, and Tamar.

PROLOGUE

AUGUST SNAPPED ITS SUSPENDERS against a proud chest of Santa Ana heat. Laboring against the invisible oppression of weather, I sprinkled aromatherapy oils on my clean bed linens and smoothed a pillowcase. When I bent down to gather the dirty sheets, I glanced toward the white ruffled bed skirt and saw a rattlesnake staring back at me.

Now, what I knew about snakes you could hold in one hand—preferably an unbitten one. But it doesn't take much to know a rattler when you see one.

I looked at the specimen coiled about two feet away on my bedroom floor. He had cocoa diamonds along his back, blotches of taupe on his sides, and a definite pit viper head. I looked at his rattle. It wasn't shakin', but I was.

When the snake looked up at me, he saw a solid woman old enough to experience the occasional hot flash yet young enough to boogie. He saw thick chestnut hair with a few strands of silver. My ethnic print blouse belied remnants of my hippie days; the denim cutoffs just said it was Saturday. In all, I saw a handsome but dangerous snake; the snake saw a handsome but daunted woman.

Watching *National Geographic*, I can appreciate the beauty of snakes and their role in the ecosystem, but when they take me by surprise in my bedroom, I find my attitude less enlightened. I put one foot gingerly behind the other and started to back out of the room.

Suddenly the snake's tail vibrated like a cicada with Parkinson's. I stopped; quieted my breathing. The snake was between me and the phone on my nightstand; I couldn't reach it. The tail stopped rattling. As beads of perspiration dripped down my cleavage, I inched backward again.

When I was out of striking range, I hurried the last few steps, closed the door behind me, and raced for the phone in the kitchen. Three button punches later, I was telling the dispatcher my problem. "Help! Right away! Someone tried to kill me with a rattlesnake!"

I won't bore you with the dispatcher's calm and tedious interrogation (I can just see the Help Wanted ad for that position: "Must have disposition cooler than William Buckley. Lack of human empathy a plus"), but eventually I understood two things: She was sending Animal Control to deal with the snake, and she didn't believe it was a murder attempt.

But I did. What hills are to San Francisco, canyons are to San Diego: They rise; we dip. The canyons enable us to live in a metropolis, battling traffic jams and enjoying the fine arts, yet never be more than minutes from hawks, coyotes, raccoons, lizards, possums, skunks, owls, foxes, and yes, snakes. But these wild animals, except for the occasional possum or skunk, don't often venture into our residential neighborhoods—they have too many canyons to choose from. There's little reason for a rattlesnake to enter a home in an established residential neighborhood four full blocks from the nearest canyon entrance.

I wasn't satisfied with the dispatcher's reassurances. Standing in the hallway outside my bedroom, I cracked open the door. The rattler hadn't moved. Keeping an eye on the snake, I called the only cop I knew personally, Kari Dixon, a detective serving as a hate crimes specialist on the San Diego police force. We used to date a few years ago. The break-up was more like a wind-down at my request; we'd spoken only intermittently since.

"Kari, it's Tess," I began, trying to contain my anxiety long enough for social niceties.

"Long time, no hear from. What's up, girl?"

"Someone put a rattlesnake in my bedroom!" I blurted. Silence on the other end of the line. Not the reaction I'd expected. I continued, "You there?"

"I was waiting for the punch line. This is one of your phallic jokes, right?"

"Of course not! He was so close I saw my life pass before my eyes!" OK, a slight exaggeration.

"Are you bitten?"

"No, but . . ."

"Call Animal Control; they'll get rid of it for you."

"Animal Control's on the way. I just thought the police might want to know someone tried to kill me." I paused for effect. "You remember the kid who lives across the street from me—Smacker?"

"Rap star wannabe. Yeah, nice kid."

"He told me that Mrs. LaQuinta—she lives two doors down—her cat was killed by a strange snake about a week ago."

"Was the snake in the house?"

"No, out in the garden, but . . ."

I heard stifled laughter. "What kind of snake was it?" Kari asked.

"Smacker wasn't sure. The LaQuinta's vet said the toxin didn't match any of the rattlers that live around here. Otherwise the antidote would have worked and Mrs. LaQuinta would still have her cat."

"Did they find the snake?"

"Well, no."

"So this cat could've been poisoned by a wasp or a tarantula or even a pesticide."

"I suppose so. But . . ."

"Rattlers live around here, girl. No reason to suspect foul play."

"So you're telling me sometimes a hiss is just a hiss?"

She laughed outright this time. "Ex-actly!" Her tone changed. "Look, if you want me to, uh, come over and check it out, um, I'm cool with . . ."

"Just document it for the files, OK?" The rattler had now slithered completely under my bed—not a vision conducive to sweet dreams.

Forty minutes later, I was sipping Tanqueray on the rocks and repeating my woes to Roland Sanchez of Animal Control. "I don't understand why they sent *you*, no offense. This is a homicide attempt; the cops should be here!"

Roland's intelligent eyes caught mine and he smiled. He picked up the trap box near my dresser. I heard the snake inside the box slide with the motion. Not for the first time Roland patiently explained, "This is a Southern Pacific rattler, native to coastal San Diego. It's scorching today; probably just came in for the shade."

The conversation sputtered a few more minutes until Roland nonchalantly placed the trap box in the back of his Animal Control truck and pulled away. I secured all the doors and windows, turned on a fan, and lay my head down on a pillow fragrant with lavender and peppermint.

My emotionally drained, heat-sapped body wanted to nap. But my gin-inspired mind kept seeing snakes on the movie screen of my closed eyelids. It was rational to believe the house was now snake-free, but rational or not, above the drone of the fan I imagined hisses and sensed surreptitious movements.

I gave up on the nap, poured myself another gin, and considered the situation. I'd been home doing chores all day; no one had been near the house. I'd had my bedroom slider open to the back patio. And maybe this particular rattler had a poor sense of 'hood. Whether it was the comfort of liquor or logic, I started to calm down. I put an old Eagles CD on the stereo. Eagles kill snakes, something the Mexican flag, seen frequently in our border town, graphically reminds us.

When I'm not sharing my house with a rattlesnake, I share it with my housemate, Lana Maki. Finnish, Lapp, and Norwegian, she looks like a blonde-haired, blue-eyed Asian—as much an oxymoron as dry ice, English gourmet, and gentle laxatives. The blonde effectively camouflages her gray and her willowy figure makes her look younger than her forty-some years.

We used to be more than housemates; operative words, "used to be." Maki means 'hill' in Finnish, and years ago I had climbed her hills and explored her valleys. She eventually decided that, for her, lesbianism was a two-year sprint, not a lifetime marathon, and set her Nikes in pursuit of *hetero sapiens*. We've been platonic housemates ever since—for mutual financial benefit, for safety, for love. That such love no longer extends to connubial kisses and G-spot joys was beside the point. Almost.

I share my home with two dogs, too: Raj, my noble Welsh terrier and all-round good sport, who no doubt would have warned me of the serpentine invader; and Pookie, Lana's dachshund. Pookie could have single-handedly inspired the phrase 'dumb animal.' She walks into chair legs. She forgets her name. She's constantly underfoot. Pookie probably would've brought a toy for the rattler to play with, if Lana hadn't taken her and Raj to get their nails clipped.

Why would a rattler prefer the shade in my Mission Hills bedroom when local canyons offered snug rocks under shady trees? Roland Sanchez said it happens. Shit happens, too, but you don't want it under your bed skirt.

1

TWO BIRDS

"HE'S GONE!"

"*You sure he's the only one assigned to this area?*" *the woman asked.*

Her companion answered, "The budget cuts help; the university can't afford enough security cops. He won't be back this way for fifteen or twenty minutes." He looked at the woman carefully. "You ready?"

Silently, she nodded.

The man parked the car as close as possible on the grass, where tread marks wouldn't show. He left the motor running. He lifted the body from the trunk and the woman grabbed other items they needed.

When the palm fronds were in place, the man laid the body down carefully. He put one gloved hand inside his jacket pocket and, in the nearly moonless night, let his fingers locate the article by its unusual texture and shape. He slipped the appendage where they wanted it and stepped back. The woman hesitated.

"*It's what we have to do,*" *he assured her.* "*It's justice.*"

The woman began her tasks. The man grew anxious. "*Hurry up with the buttons,*" *he urged.*

"*OK, OK,*" *his cohort replied. She finished their distribution and took one last look at the corpse.*

"*Brush away any footprints,*" *he reminded her on the way back.*

As she opened the car door, she paused and stared up at the night sky. "*With all the clues we're providing,*" *she said,* "*you really think they'll look for footprints?*"

2

CRIMINITLIES

THE EVENING WAS A COOL WET sponge of promise. I love autumn; I took my first breaths in early October. For three days after I was born, my survival was threatened by lung problems. Live or die—that is always the question, whether something's rotten in Denmark, wheezing in Jersey, or aromatic in San Diego. Tonight, mouth-watering smells rose from the stove.

Our kitchen is oblong and narrow, running from the dining room to the back porch, with an alcove used as a breakfast nook. We've painted the old-fashioned wooden cabinets and drawers many times; I took in their current combo of cornflower blue and yellow. Potholders, dishtowels, and artwork tickled the color theme across the room.

We'd already eaten dinner; I was preparing my contribution to a potluck lunch at work tomorrow. I reached across Lana for the oregano. Lana, putting away dishes near the spice rack, looked at me with disbelief. "Oregano, too?"

"Oregano tastes great in pasta sauce."

"But you already put in garlic and onion. There'll be too many flavors."

"You're Finnish. When it's time to fricassee reindeer, I'll consult you," I teased.

"Not everyone can be Italian."

"And the taste buds and beds of the world mourn that fact." I'm half-Jewish and half-Italian, but when I'm cooking or making love, you'd think I just arrividerci'd from Roma.

Lana turned the burner on under the kettle for a late cup of chamomile tea.

Rap! Rap! Rap! A fist that meant business pounded our front door. At this hour of night, it probably wasn't a neighbor with a knock-knock joke. I hushed Raj and Pookie, flicked on the porch light, and looked through the security peephole. Sergeant Kari Dixon stood on my front porch.

I opened the door and in walked the slight, scrappy woman with whom I'd had a brief affair. She had skin the color of dried sycamore leaves, eyes like the bottom of a stream, and could pass for Rosie Perez's sister. "Kari! Come on in."

"Hey. I know it's late, but I need to talk to you. Official business." She and Lana exchanged a nod of minimal social acknowledgement. I'd dated Kari shortly after Lana and I broke up. Kari claimed that the sexual tension between Lana and me buzzed like not-to-code wiring in an ungrounded house. At the time, it probably did. That did not increase Kari's fondness for Lana. Lana felt there were too many guns and authority figures in the world and she didn't particularly want them in her home, so the antipathy was mutual.

Raj offered Kari a friendly Woof! then lay down near the fireplace to watch the main event. Kari moved across our gumdrop-colored Guatemalan rug and settled on the cream leather couch. Pookie rubbed against her ankles in an attempt to ingratiate.

"My business relates to you, Tess." She gave Lana a look that said "disappear." Lana calmly returned the look and stayed. Kari shifted her weight and said, "There's been a murder; a woman's body was discovered on UCSD campus this morning. Maybe you heard it on the news?"

I hadn't heard anything about a murder. "I was at work all day and I didn't watch the news this evening."

"A teacher found the body this morning before classes started. It's a ritualistic-looking crime scene; the victim was a lesbian. We may have a hate murderer, a serial killer, or both on our hands."

I heard an intake of breath from Lana's direction. "Sounds awful, Kari. Jeez. But what's this got to do with me?" I asked. I noticed my voice mimicked her somber tone.

The kettle shrilled. Lana rose. "Tea? We've got Earl Grey, chamomile, spice?" she asked Kari. She didn't bother asking me; she knew I was a java junkie.

"Coffee if you have it. If not, water's fine," Kari replied.

Lana left for the kitchen. Kari turned back to me. "Need you to look at some photos taken at the crime scene. You know this woman?"

She handed me several pictures. The first two were side angle shots taken from about twelve feet away. They showed a woman's body lying on a bed of palm fronds on a slate bench. The bench sat along a winding tiled footpath. Having taken a few courses at UCSD, I recognized it immediately as the Snake Path, part of the school's outdoor art collection. The head of the tiled snake begins at the main library terrace and twists its way for another 500 feet through the campus. Along the way the snake meanders around a little garden representing Eden. The slate bench sat within this mini-Eden.

The victim had short gray hair and a trim build. She wore a red T-shirt, blue jeans, and sneakers. She looked like an older student, peacefully snoozing. No blood, no sign of struggle.

Lana returned with our drinks. I put those two photos on the coffee table for her to look at and studied the next one. This was a much closer shot, taken by someone standing over the body. "What the hell?"

Kari grimaced. "Yeah, this guy's twisted."

A variety of old buttons decorated the T-shirt. Human hairs of different lengths and colors interspersed the buttons. A slight smudge of some sort appeared on her forehead.

"Do you know her?" Kari asked again.

"Not personally, but I worked with her a couple of years in the Pride Parade. The Gay Veterans contingent. Two Marines told me she helped them for months; even paid some of their legal tab so they could manage honorable discharges. Everyone seemed to like her a lot. Can't remember her name."

"Belle Farby. Sixty-one. Divorced." Kari's voice fought something as she continued. "She's retired navy, lived in Point Loma. She didn't have any connection with UCSD. She and her partner, Darlene Nealson, been together thirty years. Darlene reported her missing last night."

Kari played anxiously with the beads in her dreadlocks. "Inside her jeans pocket was a snake's rattle."

Lana's spoon clattered to the floor. I re-inspected the picture.

Kari lifted her eyes from the floor and looked at us. "Keep that to yourselves," she instructed firmly. "The business about the rattle—we're holding that from the media. No one else knows."

"Criminitlies!" I exclaimed. It's a word I heard frequently from my Jersey relatives. I have no idea what it means; it just comes out sometimes, like now, as a sickening realization flushed through me. Lesbians. Snakes. Phallic symbols. Penis envy. I got up from the couch and paced. Part of a rattlesnake. I now understood why Kari had knocked on my door.

Kari downed some coffee. "You had this rattlesnake thing happen and you're a lesbian; now a woman gets murdered with a rattlesnake and she's a lesbian. Maybe coincidence, but probably not."

"Now I get the significance of the Snake Path," I commented.

"Are you sure she was murdered?" Lana asked. Kari and I stared at her. She continued, "I mean, I don't see any wounds. How was it done?"

"There are two puncture marks on her neck. You can't see them in these photos," Kari answered.

"Lana, snakes don't crawl into people's pockets, lop off their own tails, and commit herpetological hari kari," I added. "It's murder all right."

Pookie had lodged herself in the space between the couch and the coffee table. Kari rose and stepped over her. "When you called me in late August, I was sure the snake crawled in by itself . . . Anyway, Tess, I'm sorry I didn't pay more attention."

"Are we still in danger?" Lana wanted to know.

Kari scratched Pookie on the nose. "Hard to say. The snake thing still could be coincidence. We'll have extra patrols in your neighborhood. Lock your doors and windows. Be careful. You've got two dogs; that helps." She put her hand on the doorknob and turned to me. "I need you to come down to the station tomorrow around three and give us more information. Might be a link between you and Belle Farby. If we can find that link, maybe we find our perp."

I walked Kari out to her car. "So, how're you doing, besides dealing with this? The kids OK?" Kari's son and daughter were sun and moon in her emotional universe. With a job that meant the world to her, I'd been left in the asteroid belt when we were dating.

"Hunter had so many ear infections this year, he had to have tubes put in his ears at Children's. It really helped. Simone's growing like a weed. I haven't been dating much; no time. But I'm hanging in there."

"Yeah, me too. So far, anyway. Well, see you tomorrow."

After Kari left, I helped Lana load cups and saucers in the dishwasher.

"So what do you think?" I asked her.

"I think it's a bad idea to date cops."

"We just heard about a ritual murder and you're focused on my love life?"

"It looked like she was laid out. Like a viewing."

"A viewing with buttons and hair on her shirt and a snake's rattle in her pocket?"

She shrugged. "It just doesn't have the right aura." She dried her hands on a towel and headed toward her bedroom.

Lana's rarely met a New Age notion she didn't like. My mind tends toward healthy skepticism, logic algorithms, and planting both feet on terra firma. While I embrace the un-solved or misunderstood, I don't believe in astrology, Ouija boards, crop circles, or auras.

"'Doesn't have the right aura'?" I muttered to myself as I finished cleaning up. "We got a class-A psycho out there threatening lesbians and she's worried about the victim's halo. Auras, right. Kiss my ass!"

Lana stuck her head into the kitchen. "No, you'd enjoy that too much!"

I blushed and wiped up a dab of pasta sauce from the stove. Maybe I *will* go lighter on the seasonings. Life seems spicy enough.

3

IMITECH. UATECH?

WHAT IF FRIDA KAHLO had gone into dry cleaning? Or Mother Teresa into architecture? As I snapped nylon shades against my car windshield the next morning in the Imitech parking lot, I thought how important it is to match the right talent to the right teacup.

It took me years to make peace with earning a paycheck. I had many interests in life, none of which the world was inclined to pay me for pursuing. After false starts in a Bible college, real estate, the navy, and a hodgepodge of other jobs, I finally wedged my history-turned-math-major degree into a database slot that fit.

Imitech Foundation is a subsidiary of a much publicized software titan. We're essentially a tax write-off for our parent company, donating Web design, programming, and engineering to charitable causes. We share a building with a satellite manufacturer and a firm that specializes in the computerized design of the dimples on golf balls. Maybe they moonlighted Buzz Lightyear's chin.

I booted up, filled my Kwakiutl totem coffee mug, and launched into the arcane rites of Perl scripts and SQL searches. Morning passed quickly and soon we were feasting on the goodies we'd brought for the October birthday potluck.

There was the usual nearly naughty birthday card and a moist devil's food cake as well as red potato salad, sliced ham, and fresh strawberries. Despite Lana's misgivings, my pasta dish was well received.

I was savoring the clove smell from the ham and contemplating one more morsel of cake when my boss, Walker Boniface, approached. A few years younger than me, Walker is the kind of guy you'd enjoy sitting next to in a bar. He picked up this morning's *San Diego Union* from a lunchroom table. The morning paper had disclosed Belle Farby's sexual preference. Walker observed, "There's a lot they're not telling us about this. You know anything about it, Tess?"

"Why would I know something? I was here at work all day yesterday, remember?" I felt the spotlight, a natural consequence of my role as token lesbian in a small work group. If anything happened to any lesbian within a three-state radius, I was supposed to know the scuttlebutt. And in fact, I did know more than I let on.

Soon Walker glanced at his watch. We had miles to code before we leave.

The potluck broke up the day. Only an hour later, my silver Infiniti FX and I successfully dodged the Poopalong Cassidy in front of us on I-5 as I headed south toward police headquarters.

Regrettably, city freeways are rarely carefree ways. At rush hour they have all the flow of the 'before' pipe in a Drano ad. But heading downtown at 2:10 P.M., I-5 was as open as a brothel on Saturday night. Very soon, the early Friday work traffic would set in, but right now I had Mission Bay Park to my right, Spanish architecture and palm trees to my left, and no black-and-whites behind me. I revved the engine up to eighty-five miles per hour. The tachometer crept upward almost as fast as the corners of my mouth.

Eight elated minutes later, I took the Civic Center exit and juked my way through traffic to Broadway. Stoplight by stoplight I passed brick boarding houses, sailors on street corners, the gentrified Gaslamp Quarter, ninety-nine cent stores, winos, Randian office towers, and the art déco Horton Plaza. Downtown San Diego is as homogenous as ethnicity in Brooklyn.

I found a parking space on Fifteenth Street, walked into the police station, and told the woman at the front desk I was there to see Detective Kari Dixon. Her nose formed a little kink. Knowing that anyone working the front desk of a metropolitan police station sees all kinds of human tortellini, I found it hard not to take offense. Then I realized she probably knew which case Kari was working on. I guess anyone affiliated with a lesbian snake murder raises even cynical eyebrows.

While I waited, I wondered. Was some sicko murdering lesbians and planting snake rattles in their pockets as a mockery? Or was it just happenstance that Belle was a lesbian? Maybe her killer hated all women. Maybe some woman had

Bobbittized him and now he was seeking revenge. Maybe snakes were somehow related to Belle's work or hobbies. Surely her partner of thirty years would know such things.

My mental gyrations were disrupted by a direct hit to my reptilian brain: smell. Pungent body odor wafted from a wild-eyed homeless woman clothed entirely in purple who'd wandered into the station. Once upon a time she'd been someone's little girl. Sugar and spice, and everything nice; that's what little girls are made of. And little boys? Snakes . . .

4

THROUGH
THE VILEDUCT

DARLENE NEALSON CONVEYED a feline economy of movement. Her large hazel eyes practically lasered intelligence. Red hair, past its prime, softened her face. Grief bore down on her shoulders, lending the air of those lonely women on buses no one wants to sit next to. She was at least a decade younger than her mate, and well preserved.

Kari had introduced us, brought coffee, and made us as comfortable as the gray metal chairs, Formica table, and windowless room would allow. "Tess, I've explained to Ms. Nealson—"

"Darlene," Nealson interjected.

Kari nodded and continued, "—to Darlene why you're here. I need you two to go over daily activities, memberships in organizations, lifestyle patterns, and so forth, to see if we can find any overlap. Darlene, why don't you start with Wednesday morning, the day Belle disappeared?"

"Um, Wednesday Belle and I slept in late." Darlene glanced down at some low profile truth. I wondered if they'd made love that final morning. She continued, "Belle got up, put the coffee on, and went to get us some bagels for brunch. I remember . . ." Her voice broke and she started to sob. The pain in the small room narrowed the walls.

Kari motioned for Darlene to continue.

Darlene spoke so softly I had to lean forward to hear her. "Before she left she said she had to stop at the ATM; she needed cash. She might have gone to the bank."

"Oh, man, sorry, I meant to tell you," Kari sputtered. "We found her Toyota in a small strip mall, across the parking lot from a branch of Union Bank."

Darlene turned her piercing, perceptive eyes on me. My heart tightened in my chest. "*Now* they go looking for her car! When I called and reported her missing, they were too busy to look for it! She just went to run some errands and never . . . never came back!" Like certain Harry Potter jellybeans, she was bile bitter.

Kari defended the police. "It's been policy forever: We don't look for adults missing less than forty-eight hours."

I thought Kari could've been a bit more sympathetic. Darlene just glared. Maybe she'd once been a smoker; something about her still smoldered. I broke in. "I use Union Bank, too. Might be something there, but I doubt it."

Kari wrote it down anyway. "What branch?"

"The Hillcrest branch, on Fifth Avenue."

"Could be some staffer works at both Hillcrest and Point Loma branches. We'll check it out," she said, making notes. "OK, keep going. What about hobbies? Sports? Activities?"

Darlene offered, "We liked to bike—not mountain biking, but long rides on Imperial Beach Strand."

Kari gave her an encouraging smile. "Good. What else? Are you active in the lesbian community?"

"Only the Gay Veterans in the Pride Parade. Otherwise, we're homebodies. Belle took early retirement from the navy, so she could stay home to take care of Milt."

"Milt?" I asked.

"Her dad. He had Huntington's." Darlene must have known by our look that we didn't recognize the illness. "Woodie Guthrie's disease," she clarified. "Anyway, Belle's mom died years earlier and Belle didn't want to put him in a nursing home, so Milt lived with us. We had an aide come in part-time, but it kept us pretty housebound. He passed away last June. We were just beginning to have some time to ourselves."

Part of what makes us fully human is caring for our elderly. While Belle and Darlene's lifestyle seemed a little bland, it also sounded fundamentally decent.

Kari probed again. "Volunteer work? Organizations?"

"Belle delivered Meals on Wheels on Tuesday nights." Darlene's voice broke, but she regained her composure.

Kari looked at me inquiringly. I shrugged. "I don't bike much; haven't worked with Meals on Wheels. I *was* in the navy."

Darlene continued. "I work the evening shift at City Medical Center, so we spend . . . used to spend . . . most days together. We'd garden, read out back by the patio, go to movies."

Kari asked, "Did you or Belle ever have any snakes as pets?"

Darlene snapped. "This borders on harassment! You've asked me that three times before! Belle had allergies. We didn't have *any* pets, let alone snakes!"

Kari let it go, then took down the name of every theater, club, place of worship, grocery store, and professional service (doctor, lawyer, plumber, auto mechanic) first in Belle's life, then in mine. The only commonalities were Union Bank and the U.S. Navy. With tens of thousands of Union Bank customers in San Diego and millions of navy veterans, these weren't the hottest leads for a murder investigation.

A young cop with no hair and a five o'clock shadow opened the door and said, "'Scuse me, Sergeant Dixon. They said you'd want to see this as soon as it was in." He handed Kari a folder stamped MEDICAL EXAMINER'S REPORT, regarded us with undisguised curiosity, and left.

Kari scanned the paperwork. With some gentleness she said, "Darlene, the autopsy shows that Belle was not sexually molested in any way."

Darlene let out a whimper. Can we feel threads of relief within a tapestry of sorrow?

Culling points from the autopsy notes, Kari shared more information. The tone of her voice once again grew cool. "The body had been bathed and dressed post-mortem. Time of death is only approximate because Belle's body clearly had been transported from wherever she was murdered to the UCSD Snake Path; we don't know if her body was in a warm or cold place before that. Best they can tell us is she probably died between eleven A.M. and four P.M. Wednesday."

"Did she suffer?" Darlene choked out.

"I'm not a medical expert but from what I see here, I don't think so. Not long anyway. They think death occurred in less than five minutes." Kari put the notes down and looked at both of us. "There was no rattlesnake venom in her body. She died from a much stronger toxin. They're running something called an ELISA 'immuno-sorbent assay'. . ." she stumbled a bit on the phrase, ". . . venom detection kit. Lab says it might take a while to identify it."

Darlene looked like she was trying to read the Pledge of Allegiance in a bowl of alphabet soup. Nothing made sense.

"At least it makes your job easier," I told Kari. "Obviously your killer is someone who can obtain and handle deadly snakes. Someone from the zoo?"

"Maybe, but right now we don't even know if the toxin that killed her is snake venom. We've started a preliminary investigation; interviewed herpetologists at the zoo. But San Diego's also got the Wild Animal Park, native rattlesnakes, hobbyists, SDSU zoology majors. If the toxin is from some kind of sea creature, throw in Scripps and Sea World, too. And Petco's headquartered here—they cater to dozens of local snake owners. The snake lead isn't as promising as it sounds."

Darlene started to shiver. "I'm freezing." She stood up and rubbed her arms to warm and calm herself.

I looked at her. "You're scared."

Honest vulnerability met my eyes. "Terrified."

I pulled my light windbreaker from the back of my chair and offered it to her. She put the jacket around her shoulders and pulled herself into it.

"Guns are pretty effective against both snakes and people," I suggested.

"I *hate* guns! Belle had a pistol while she was in the navy. I made her get rid of it when she retired. I won't allow guns in my home."

I could guess who wore the pants in their family, probably because she more often wore the skirts.

Kari reassured her. "We'll have extra patrols in your
neighborhood."

Darlene gestured toward me and asked Kari, "Do you
still think what happened to this woman is related somehow?
She doesn't really seem to have much in common with me
and Belle."

This woman? Not much in common? I somehow felt
jilted.

"We just don't know yet. To be on the safe side, I'm issu-
ing a warning through the Gay and Lesbian Community
Center, asking women to be on the alert." Kari closed her
notebook. "Thanks for your cooperation, both of you. If
you think of anything else, get in touch."

Pheromones from fear and evil permeated the station
halls, creating a vileduct of human pain for Darlene and me
to navigate. The soft gray of the textured walls was probably
meant to be soothing; nevertheless, when we finally passed
through the front door I savored the fresh air.

Darlene headed out along the front plaza and down the
block without so much as a backward glance. My eyes followed her until she climbed into a blue Subaru Forester.

Kari walked up beside me. "I wouldn't get too involved
with her if I were you. In any murder case, we look close to
home; see what's what."

"Yesterday you were sure this was the work of some mad
serial killer or hate criminal. What's with you?"

"Coroner's report changes things. When a body's been
cleaned and dressed, it can mean the perp had a relationship
with the victim. Maybe even an intimate relationship." Kari

squinted into the sun. "I hope Harry was thorough. Our pathologist is so close to retirement, he's got one foot out the door. Anyway, I spent a long time today grilling Darlene before you got here, girl, and she's got no alibi for the time of the murder. Says she fell back to sleep and when she woke up and Belle was gone, she called their friends. When no one had heard from Belle, Darlene notified us, just before she left for her evening shift."

"Do you really believe she killed her lover of thirty years?"

Kari circumvented an answer. "She'll be a suspect till we clear her. You know what she does for a living?"

I tried to recall. "Hospital work of some sort?"

"She's a surgical nurse. I'm going to ask the M.E. if those puncture wounds could be needle marks instead of fang marks. Meanwhile, I've ordered a psych profile based on the crime scene to try to see what we're dealing with. What's your take?"

"I think Darlene Nealson's in a world of hurt."

I wanted to help that hurt go away. Darlene and I now shared an intense involuntary intimacy. We knew things about each other strangers shouldn't know. Since I was already involved and since my own safety might be at stake, I made a promise to myself to find out what really happened. It was a significant decision, one with implications for my time and resources.

Little did I know how much practice I'd soon get making life and death decisions.

5

GRAVY LADLE SMILE

WHEN I CAME HOME, AS SOON as I stepped out of my car I heard yowling and yipping. Oh, God! Was Raj confronting a snake? Was Lana in danger? I dashed into the house.

As I entered, Lana closed the sunporch door firmly behind her, quieted the dogs, and gave me a warm welcome hug. "How was your day?" she asked. There are hugs and then there are *hugs*. This sudden affection took me quite by surprise. Her voice resonated like a plucked wildflower behind the ear of a child—gentle yielding entwined with feral beauty.

I answered neutrally, went to the kitchen, and pulled a cherry ginger beer from the fridge. I tried to glimpse the sunporch but Lana managed subtly to block my view.

The moment the ladle emerges from the bowl, full of homemade gravy destined for *your* plate; the stunning giddiness at the top of the Ferris wheel; the smell of your mother's skin—Lana gave me a smile that encompassed them all. "I have a little favor to ask, Tess."

"Yes?"

"You know Project Wildlife sometimes needs to place injured animals in people's homes while they heal. Well, I did some volunteer work there today and . . ." She cracked the sunporch door open a few inches. "We need some place to keep *him*."

In a corner of the room, inside a cage, sat the biggest damn raccoon I've ever seen. I'm talking big enough to compete in the World Wrestling Federation. His right rear foot was bandaged. The dogs went ballistic again until Lana calmed them. She closed the sunporch door and joined me in the kitchen.

"Um, don't you think Raj and Pookie are just a tad upset over this house guest?"

"Yes, ordinarily they wouldn't place a raccoon in a home with dogs, but it's sort of an emergency. The family who usually handles raccoons is on vacation. The other woman who's qualified for raccoons broke her arm playing tennis and can't take care of him. This little guy just needs a safe place to hole up for a few days . . . just till Monday night. Please? The kids will settle down once they get used to him."

We all know about the power of exes to make us cry "why?" In my heart of hearts, I've given up tomorrow but not forever. "I suppose we can adapt for a few days."

She laid a lesser hug on me and started for the sunporch. I was thinking up a name for the raccoon when Lana turned back toward me. "Oh, I almost forgot. A woman at the Project told me that the whole county had incidents with snakes and other wildlife last August. There was an earthquake near the Salton Sea on the thirtieth. Maybe the animals were reacting to their internal seismo-thingies."

"You think the rattlesnake in our house was just a coincidence?" I asked.

She nodded. "Animals act strange right before earthquakes. They pick up vibrations. Maybe the snake was feeling out of sorts and came in the house, not realizing what he'd gotten himself into. Maybe he felt more protected indoors."

Well, it was a theory; perhaps a good one. I nicknamed the raccoon Fess, for Fess Parker of *Davy Crockett* TV fame—the one who wore a coonskin cap. Not very PC, but then when have I ever worried about that? Bidding farewell to Fess, I changed into my favorite gray sweats and a T-shirt. I took the dogs out for a block orbit then made myself steamed zucchini with cilantro-lime sauce and a buffalo burger. I eat lean, low fat buffalo burgers so I can put as much teriyaki or steak sauce on them as I want without guilt. Or with less guilt, anyway.

Guilt seems to me a contrary emotion, slipping into crevices where it doesn't belong, avoiding corridors it should visit. It nags me with concern about the fat content of my dinner, but so rarely stings the conscience of murderers.

6

WALKING
THE DOGS

FEW PLEASURES—MAYBE FIREFLIES, Mozart concertos, and harvest moons—rank as high for me as that first cup of coffee in the morning. On the Indian summer Saturday morning after Kari interviewed me and Darlene, I moved from bedroom to kitchen in sweet anticipation.

A frying pan sizzled with burned butter and egg, and the kitchen smelled funky. I turned off the burner. Raj hasn't yet been known to cook his own meals, so I looked around for Lana. Kitchen, dining room, living room, hallway, her bedroom. No trace. The bathroom—fragrant with herbal hair conditioner, Shea butter, and damp terry towels—was empty.

Lana credited Shea butter for preserving her skin. The smell of it triggered memories. Being platonic housemates worked most of the time but lately I'd been *in the mood*. Every once in a while, she still wagged the tail of my Lassie.

I retraced my path to the kitchen and brewed up some of Kenya's finest. I got the dogs fresh water and a little dry food, not sure if Lana had already fed them.

A blur of motion caught my eye. Lana stood there on our patio, hair wet, in only her pajama bottoms, staring in fascination at the liquid amber tree in our backyard. She jumped when she saw me and crossed her arms in front of her. "Tess!"

"Your eggs are burning," I said, glimpsing two over easy.

"I started breakfast and I just stepped out to let the sun help dry me off. You know how much I like the smell of the morning air . . . then my eye caught these little pokey balls, or burrs, seedpods, whatever. I mean, I'd seen them before, but I'd never really *looked* . . . well . . ." She darted into her bedroom and returned wearing blue jeans and a white blouse with lace trim.

I spread peanut butter on wheat toast and ate hungrily. I sipped my coffee. "You're up early for Saturday."

"I teach Qi Gong at ten, give a massage at twelve-thirty, then teach Tai Chi at three."

I've known Lana since she was 106 in frog years, but she still holds many secrets. We were eating a Sunday brunch of Brie and chocolate-dipped pears at a restaurant a few weeks ago when she let it slip that she never pays income tax. Apparently some crinkle in the law says if an employer pays you below a certain amount, they don't have to file a 1099 on you. She has a steady stream of employers who pay her a dollar less than the reportable criterion. As far as the government's concerned, Lana has no income. Thus, no tax. She teaches Tai Chi and Qi Gong, presents herb workshops, and does massages. She holds all the appropriate credentials for these endeavors. Since I've known her, she's worked for the Y, women's shelters, fitness clubs, private clientele, hospitals, hospices, and veterinarians. Even though I'm her housemate, I never know where she will be on any given day.

"Going out tonight?" I asked.

"No, I'll be beat. Maybe I'll watch a movie," she replied as she scraped burnt egg off the frying pan. "What are you up to?"

"Got some errands to run. Tonight I thought I'd use the Old Globe theater tickets you gave me for my birthday. I'm going to see *Of Kin and Kismet*."

"You taking Lee Anne?" she asked.

"None other." Lee Anne was a woman I dated occasionally. We weren't in love but we provided each other an acceptable sexual outlet. I don't know why I felt compelled to defend my behavior to Lana but I did. "I haven't done the wild thing in almost five weeks. I need to take my libido puppy out for a walk."

Lana smiled to herself. "That's your Mars in Scorpio." She tousled my hair on her way out of the kitchen. "If you don't make it home tonight, I'll walk the other pups."

7

THE DOOR TRICK

WHILE LANA WAS CHANNELING Chi and massaging muscles, I worked out at the gym and went grocery shopping. When I returned home, Raj kissed my face. Like a metronome on speed, his tail thumped against me in a starburst of joy. My soul smiled back at his and asked about his day. He told me he'd discovered the remnants of a thoroughly rotten avocado in the backyard and how much fun that was to play with. And here I thought he'd been drinking from the toilet again.

I rolled around with Raj a while, put away the groceries, built a scaffold with my Tinker Toys (What can I tell you? It's something I do), until it was time to get ready for my date. I needed a light dinner and a shower before I picked her up. I rummaged through the fresh groceries I'd brought home and decided on endive, feta, and walnut salad with leftover Cheesy Bread. Now that is a well-balanced meal: the salad makes you feel virtuous; the bread satisfies your taste buds.

I was savoring the remnants of the meal when I heard the critters greet Lana at the front door. Before I could exhale, Raj skittered across the kitchen floor and homed in on Pookie's food bowl like a guided missile. He began snarfing down a few stray bits.

"Raj!" I'd caught Raj playing the Door Trick on Pookie a few months ago. Raj would suddenly run to the front door and bark earnestly for about ten seconds. By then Pookie, who had heard no one, would join him and become distracted by the stranger at the door. Raj would then race into the kitchen and eat Pookie's food. Sometimes he played this trick on Pookie even when her food bowl was empty, just for kicks, I suppose.

Raj absented himself with a satisfied glint, and I started my shower. While I was there Lana really did come home, because when I emerged, she was stretched out on the living room sofa wearing pajamas, CD headphones, and cucumber slices over her eyes. She was moving to her music. I mimed to ask her what she was listening to, but realized that she couldn't see me mime with veggies on her eyelids any more than she could hear me through the headphones. I was invisible and inaudible; for a few moments, I had super powers.

I returned to the kitchen, took a cherry tomato, sliced it almost in half, and scooped out some of its pulp. I laid it on a paper towel and cleaned up after myself.

Back in my room, I laid out a pair of pleated herringbone dress slacks, a tailored black silk blouse, white suspenders, and a pair of black boots with silver chains I'd bought recently at Boot World. My figure leans more toward Sophia Loren than Sophia Petrillo, and suspenders on a buxom woman send messages. I tucked my blouse into the slacks, adjusted my suspenders, and went out to play Instant Messenger.

Before I left I retrieved the cherry tomato from the kitchen, walked over to Lana and fit it over her nose. I focused the Polaroid and got off one excellent shot of the cuke-eyed and tomato-nosed clown before she had time to react.

When she realized what was on her nose, Lana started to laugh in spite of herself. "Bye!" I sang as I waved the snapshot at her and vanished out the door.

It was a short ride to Lee Anne Portnoy's apartment in Little Italy, so I only had the opportunity to squirt imaginary mustard gas at two bad drivers along the way.

Lee Anne was ready on time. She's always on time. She's capable of decent conversation. She has dark chocolate eyes, flawless olive skin, teeth that could star in whitening commercials, and the shiniest black hair of any woman her age I've ever seen. And there's never a hair out of place. Why didn't I fall for her? Precisely because there's never a hair out of place. She tries too hard. And takes everything too seriously. Dating has left me cautious.

The last woman I was involved with came down from L.A. every few weeks to visit her brother and my bed. She affected some Hindu moniker like Kali Dali, but her driver's license read Linda Sue Ettelson. We'd met at a multimedia convention. A digital artist for one of Hollywood's biggest animation studios, she'd been working on a Discovery Channel dinosaur special. One evening I had the temerity to say that her job sounded fun. "Fun?" she'd asked. "I spent the last week perfecting the urine flow rate of a Suchomimus taking a whiz. Once I get that down, I can focus on the glow of the urine as it moves in a stream." We broke it off after two months.

It's hard not to enjoy an evening at the Old Globe. A faux-Tudor enclave within the Spanish architecture of Balboa Park, the theater grounds were filled with PBS types in black-and-white and well read all over. *Of Kin and Kismet* played on the Center Stage, a theater-in-the-round experience that brings you so close to the actors you can catch the tick of panic when they muff a line and have to ad lib. During intermission, Lee Anne and I stood in the theater plaza mesmerized by a huge ash tree stretching bare branches into the night sky. We sipped steaming cappuccinos but didn't talk much.

After a satisfying performance, on the drive back to Lee Anne's apartment I asked, "So how's everything been going in your life? Do you still enjoy working at the clinic?"

"Do you really want to know, or is that just social lubricant until you can bed me?"

This is the problem with dating a psychotherapist. We pulled into her driveway. I turned off the engine, got out, and opened her door. Lee Anne and I had lasted eight months now, longer than some Vegas marriages. One of the reasons we've lasted is that I could usually get Lee Anne out of her head and into bed with a few good kisses. So I said what seemed right in the moment. "Social lubricant. Let's mess around until we need the other kind."

Lee Anne grabbed me by my suspenders and pulled me into her apartment.

Candlelight spackled the walls with mood as we nearly reenacted a scene from *Monster's Ball*. Later Lee Anne straddled me, eventually collapsing against my body. I stroked the hair of this woman who took the psychological woes of others so very much to heart. Slowly, she raised herself up. Her eyes moved down to my breasts and belly. I caught something in them.

"What's wrong, baby?" I sat myself up straighter, leaning against the pillow.

"Your breast—it looks, uh, it didn't used to look like that," she stammered.

Behind her and in front of me, her bedroom mirror reflected our naked bodies. I stood up, turned on a lamp, and approached the mirror. "Show me where."

She lightly traced the lower half of my left breast. "Right here, see."

Now that I was close to the mirror and had better lighting, I did see. From my nipple on downward the skin of my left breast appeared dimpled. The breast itself looked somewhat smaller than the other side. I'd had full symmetrical breasts since puberty. I had to admit, something looked odd. I don't do breast self-exams because my breasts have felt like beanbags for years; there's no way to tell which bumps are significant. My doctor called this fibrocystic disease, attributed it to heavy coffee consumption, and said it was nothing to worry about. I stood there in front of the mirror, feeling for lumps and found one rather prominent one among the smaller ones.

"I had a mammo earlier this year, and everything was fine," I told her truthfully. I wasn't worried. I had no pain, no nipple discharge, no reason to suspect anything serious. "This is probably from last summer when I went to Jersey on vacation. The Baron—my brother Barry—took me tubing on the bay. I sat in an inner tube and he towed it behind his motorboat. The ride was ecstasy, but my breasts took a pounding. I probably irritated a mammary gland when I did that."

Lee Anne looked doubtful, but enough endorphins had saturated her that she merely tugged my hand and walked us back to bed. Monday morning I'd call to schedule another mammo just in case. Monday, Monday. But before that, Sunday. Mañana.

I felt Lee Anne's warmth near me. Tomorrow was another day. Tonight still held opportunity.

8

INSOMNIAC
SPARROWS

AT ONE TIME IN GEORGIA, Alabama, and Texas, it was legal to own a gun but not a vibrator. This, to me, explains a lot about why the South did not rise again. Although sated from my time with Lee Anne, I spent the better part of Sunday seeking a replacement for my trusty Hitachi Magic Wand vibrator. Call it preventive maintenance; its cord was beginning to fray.

After a lazy morning with Lee Anne, a drive home, shower, fresh clothes, romp time with Raj, and an inquisitive shopping tour to several venues, I found a worthy Wand. The rest of the evening I vegged out watching A&E. I noticed that the actresses in arthritis pain reliever ads appealed more than the bimbettes pushing Pepsi. I think I've hit middle age.

That night I fell asleep not to the buzz of Hitachi, but to the chatter of insomniac sparrows. Hours later, noise like a cage of hyperactive canaries chirped me to full consciousness.

It took only a moment to realize something had set off an alarm. The dogs yelped furiously. I heard Lana call "Tess!" from down the hall.

I jumped out of bed, grabbed my .22 from the nightstand drawer, snicked off the safety, and met her in the hallway. Gun drawn, I led the way as we turned on the hall lights. No one. We advanced into the living room. Curiously, Raj and Pookie were not homing in on an intruder but rather staying close to our heels.

"The smoke alarm?" asked Lana.

I nodded; it didn't sound like the burglar alarm. "Let's try the kitchen."

We turned on the kitchen and dining room lights. No smell of gas, no burners left on, no smoke. By now, my ears adapted to the blare and I thought I knew its source. I motioned to Lana. "Check the sunporch."

We locked the dogs in Lana's room and opened the porch door. There, quite unhappy with the results he had produced, was Fess. His cage was turned on its side with the door open. The sunporch's potted plants and tray tables were not in their upright position. Fess was scrambling about, his human-like hands touching everything, desperately trying to undo whatever it was he had done to cause such a racket. Telltale paw prints marked the top of a small table near the smoke alarm. The battery test button on the alarm was depressed; Lana turned it off.

"Poor little guy," she cooed to the beast who had skittered away from us.

"'Little' like Charlemagne's empire." I reset the safety on my gun.

"OK, he's a healthy size. Let's get him back in his cage."

"This sounds like a job for Superman!"

"Very funny. Go get gloves and a coat for each of us. Close the sunporch door behind you." When I returned with our anti-raccoon armor, we donned both gloves and coat and Lana orchestrated, "You come at him from that side, I'll come from the right. Walk real slow; we don't want to scare him."

By the time we had the masked marauder re-caged, even the sparrows were asleep.

9

SERPENTS IN THE GARDEN

I'M WILDLY FOND of my ex-husband. Perhaps I'm dyslesbic. When I recall the smell of Captain Spice pipe tobacco, his pinstripe shirts with starched collars, or the relief of his back massages, I ache to see him.

Roark Jurist and I met in the late seventies when we were both assigned duty at the Naval Air Station in Brunswick, Maine. Roark arrived at NAS Brunswick as a cryptographic communications technician, a very good one at that. Roark operated and maintained the crypto computers that decoded intercepted satellite messages. Roark knew what Brezhnev had for breakfast. The navy trained me as an education specialist, having rightfully surmised that I didn't care whether Brezhnev consumed chipped beef or prune Danish.

Roark and I had just one minor glitch in our relationship: sex. He'd rather have it with Harrison Ford and I'd rather have it with Meryl Streep. We married mainly to provide cover from the suspicious eyes of the Naval Investigative Service whose paranoid witch hunts led to dishonorable discharges. Could a gay man and a lesbian create a meaningful, loving marriage? Why not?

After eight years in the navy, Roark took his discharge and went to work for the NSA. Later he schmoozed his way into a position with the ultimate stealth agency, one that makes the CIA and the FBI look like, well, the CIA and the FBI. For Roark's sake, I can't use their real name, so I'll call them Immensely Powerful Government Spooks, or IPoGS, for short. They serve as a sort of Internal Affairs for spook agencies.

Roark and I followed separate breadcrumb trails through life, quietly divorcing along the way. He now worked at IPoGS headquarters in Maryland. We talked a few times a year.

Monday morning after our staff meeting, I ducked into my office, shut the door, and dialed an unlisted number. After entering two PIN codes, I heard the baritone voice that matches the Captain Spice pipe tobacco.

"Tessy, baby! What a popper! How *are* you?" His Maryisms had intensified a few degrees since we'd last spoken.

"Hello, boy toy!" I hoped he could hear the fondness in my voice as I reached out and touched him. "I'm doing great. How 'bout you?"

"I'm fine, darlin'. Say, does your heart still flutter for O-Be-Lana Kenobe?" he teased.

"Maybe a little," I mumbled. "Listen, Roark, I need a favor. A lesbian's been murdered out here and whoever murdered her might be after me, too." That piqued his interest and I related the tale of serpents in the Garden of Belle and Darlene. "You can get almost any information through IPoGS, right?"

"Pretty much, sugar."

"Could you get me the police reports on this case? I mean, without getting yourself in trouble?"

"I can probably get you the mayor's Jockeys from his laundry basket." Like the CIA, FBI, and any other intelligence agency worthy of the name, IPoGS had avoided becoming part of the Department of Homeland Security; they worked with minimal oversight.

I chuckled. "Hold off on the boxers, although they're probably more pristine than his politics, judging from the way mayoral elections go in this town. Just send everything you can find on Belle Farby and Darlene Nealson. OK?"

"Tell you what: You e-mail me those names at this address . . ." He gave me a new way to reach him and I wrote it down. "I'll send a crypto key around 1400 today. Encrypted e-mails should get to you by evening. Will that work?"

"Oh, Roark, you're such a sweetie!"

"Tell it to George Clooney!" He laughed as we hung up.

The big guns were out.

I spent the rest of the morning trying to figure out why on one particular page of a Web site the shopping cart wouldn't work. I scrutinized every bit of code repetitively. This bug was taking me too long; Euler solved Fermat's Theorem for three in less time.

The problem was, I couldn't concentrate. I had another phone call to make, one less pleasant than asking an ex-spouse to commit federal crimes as a favor.

I zapped a Healthy Choice meal in the lunchroom microwave and took my lunch back to my desk. Between the chicken and rice entrée and an apple, I located the phone number of my primary care physician and dialed it.

"Hi. I need authorization for a mammogram." After we mucked our way through the name, address, and date of birth wasteland that for some reason must be traversed every time I called, the service rep said that because I'd already had my annual mammo, the earliest she could book me was two and a half months out. I pulled on my attitudinal cowboy boots and got in the saddle. "I'm sorry, that's unacceptable. I'd like to speak to the doctor about this."

"The doctor's in with a patient."

I dug in my spurs, steered with the reins, and bounced on the HMO bronco until three phone calls later, I got a mammo appointment for Thursday.

Satisfied, I looked back at my monitor and debugged the shopping cart code in three keystrokes.

10

IN MEMORIAM OF MORRISON?

BELLE FARBY'S FUNERAL FELL on an overcast Friday afternoon, the kind of day when I feel in country western songs and think in Salinger tales. Her service was being held at Rosecrans National Cemetery on Point Loma Peninsula, a few miles from where she had lived. According to her wishes, Belle had been cremated. Kari asked me to attend her committal ceremony in case I recognized any acquaintances Belle and I had in common; Imitech approved the time off. Lana came with me so naturally we were late. Lana's sense of time configuration may be the key to decoding Stonehenge.

A whip of dampness cracked across Catalina Boulevard, the road bisecting the cemetery east and west. Rows and rows of identical white tombstones stretched over gentle slopes, holding vigil over the San Diego Bay on one side of the road, the Pacific on the other. It was as close to the Arlington National Cemetery as the West Coast could offer.

I found the entranceway, drove past a huge flagpole, and scooted into a parking space. A quick inquiry at the information office directed us to the bay side of the cemetery. We walked past crematoria, the white marble vaults set with silver rosettes. One of them would soon hold the ashes of Belle Farby's mortal coil.

We crossed the street, hurried through wrought iron gates, and turned right on a path leading to a large gazebo. Lana and I joined the other twenty or so mourners who sat there on benches. To the left of the gazebo, an extended family of black faces quietly awaited use of the space when our time was up; beyond them, nothing but graves.

The broad expanse of tombstones jarred a memory of a poem I'd learned in eighth grade. I could only recall a few intermittent lines:

> *In Flanders fields the poppies blow*
> *Between the crosses, row on row . . .*
> *We are the Dead. Short days ago*
> *We lived . . .*

Short days ago, Belle Farby went out for bagels. Short days ago, I didn't check under my bed before climbing into it.

To me, the ultimate expression of a person's need for control is how specific they make their death and burial instructions. It's—pardon the pun—a dead giveaway if you want to control things even after you die. If my theory is correct, Belle Farby was far from a control monger. No particular order of service could be discerned; people just spoke as they felt inspired. In fact, the service seemed a bit discombobulated.

I scrutinized our group. Only Kari and Darlene looked familiar. Retired male navy chiefs in uniform sat elbow to elbow with middle-aged lesbians. Interspersed, a few well-scrubbed young people paid solemn attention. Someone's cell phone rang. About half the audience rummaged through personal gear. It rang once more before someone quieted the offending machine.

When I tuned back in, a neighbor was expressing how she knew that Belle was in a better place. I wondered why there were no clergy at the service, and if Belle's ex-husband was in attendance.

As if nominating himself for the role, a paunchy retired navy chief walked to the podium and spoke about how he could always trust Belle when they'd worked together at the Naval Air Station in Pensacola. An uncertain silence passed after he sat down.

Finally Darlene activated a karaoke machine and stood at the microphone. With evident emotion, she began a soulful rendition of "Jordan Is a Hard Road to Travel", an unusual hymn I'd never heard before. The sound track of piano, guitar, bass, and tambourines provided harmonic blues progressions. That—along with her red hair—reminded me of Bonnie Raitt. I noticed a few of our neighbors softly joining in.

Darlene was finishing the final chorus, grief or the wind bringing tears to her eyes, when the sea of black faces to our left parted and a grizzled white man lumbered through, right on up to the gazebo. He grinned drunkenly and yelled,

"How'd ya like *this* trouser snake?" as he unzipped his fly and exposed himself.

I've never seen Kari move so fast.

11

TRUTH OR CONSEQUENCES

A RATTLESNAKE COILED ITSELF on Arlo George's forearm, the words "Don't Tread on Me" wrapped beneath it. Creases lined the man's forehead above Civil War eyes—one blue, one gray; both at war.

At the cemetery, I'd hoodwinked Kari into letting me tag along by saying Arlo George looked familiar to me and I needed time to place him. Kari'd been pumping coffee into him ever since she'd uncuffed him; meanwhile, she'd let me scan parts of his file. He was sixty-three, married, and had a daughter who lived in Amsterdam. He'd retired early from the Merchant Marines due to a back injury. He'd seen a lot of ports in his life as well as many burgundies and Boone's Farms.

As soon as the coffee sparked a live neural connection, George asked to call his lawyer. Somehow George managed to convince his attorney, the dapper Fred Miyamoto, to make an appearance this late on a Friday. When he arrived, the two looked at each other with the familiarity of an old married couple studying the breakfast menu at Denny's. "Why are you holding my client?" Miyamoto inquired as he handed George a can of Pepsi. George sucked half of it down in one gulp.

"Three counts: drunk and disorderly, disturbing the peace, and public lewdness. That's for starters. Your client interrupted the funeral service of Belle Farby, the woman found murdered at UCSD last week. I have more than twenty witnesses."

Miyamoto shrugged. Arlo George smoothed the whiskers along one side of his face, turned to his lawyer and asked, "Did ya know the dead woman was a lesbo?"

"Quiet, Arlo. You'll be out in an hour." He stood up.

"I don't think so, Mr. Miyamoto. I said those charges were for starters. Your client's in deep shit. There's evidence that Belle Farby's murder was a hate crime. Your boy showed up at her funeral twirling his dick and defaming—"

Arlo George grabbed Kari's arm and twisted it. "Don't call me a boy. I'm all man, sweetheart."

In a split second Kari broke his hold, wrenched his arm, knocked over what was left of his Pepsi, and got within what any culture in the world would consider his personal space. "You lay a hand on me again, dickbrain, and I'll teach you a whole new way to play Truth or Consequences. You got that?"

Arlo George belched in her face.

Muscles tensed, Kari sat back down and spoke directly to Miyamoto, who was blotting up Pepsi with a silk handkerchief. "As I was saying, your boy behaved pretty bad at the victim's funeral. And he's got a snake tattooed on his arm; snakes are a trademark of our killer. Oh, yeah, and your client lives only three blocks from the victim's home."

Miyamoto pretended to yawn. "All circumstantial. Nothing to it."

"Juries have convicted on nothing but circumstantial; ask Scott Peterson. Or David Westerfield," Kari answered.

The polished lawyer conferred with his client. "Mr. George is willing to answer questions," Miyamoto stated.

Kari clicked the ON button of a digital voice recorder. She recorded orientation info about date, time, place, parties, and circumstances, then turned back to George. "Did you know Belle Farby?"

"Is that the lesbo they were buryin'?"

"The woman whose memorial service you disrupted, yes. Did you know her?"

"Nope, can't say I did."

I could see from Kari's expression that she didn't believe him. "Then why did you go to her funeral, Mr. George?"

Arlo looked at his lawyer who nodded. "Thought it'd be a hoot—see all them pussy lickers—her honey, her friends. How many times can ya catch a show like that?"

"Why did you expose yourself?"

"I heard she was messin' with a snake; probably tryin' to do somethin' kinky with it. Everyone knows they're whad-dya call a phallic symbol. Papers were full o' stories about it. Thought maybe some o' them lesbos would like to see the real thing. I got me a real long johnson."

Kari took a deep breath. Miyamoto gave his client a warning look. Kari continued, "What bank do you use?"

George squirmed in his seat. "You're not puttin' any holds on my money, are you?" When Kari said no, he answered, "Union Bank and Wells Fargo."

"Have you ever worked with or around snakes?"

George touched his tattoo. "Got one right here, don't I?"

For benefit of the recorder, Kari said, "Mr. George indicated a rattlesnake tattoo on his right forearm. Mr. George, please answer my question."

For the first time, he seemed shaken. "Never been around snakes, no. I'm scared o' those fuckers."

"Where were you on the Wednesday before last?"

"Hell, I have no idea."

Kari gave him the evil eye. "If you don't want to be held on suspicion of murder, you better think about it. And think hard."

George shrugged. "What day was that again?"

"Wednesday, week before last."

Suddenly the microwave in George's brain beeped DONE. "Oh, oh, I remember. I was out of town; went up to Frisco for a Merchant Marine conference. Told a buncha sea stories that week, I did. Ginny can vouch for me. She phoned me while I was up there. Might still have the plane ticket at home."

"It was just called the 'Merchant Marine Conference'?"

"It was one o' the IMO meetings."

"What's IMO?"

"International Maritime Organization. Think it was the Solid Cargo Conference or somethin' like that. My wife's got the brochure at home."

Miyamoto offered an oily smile. "That should suffice, sergeant. We're going to post bail now. He kept his part of the deal."

After they left, Kari joined me in the observation room. She brought each of us a cup of coffee with cream. "I don't know which stunk worse—his breath or his personality."

"You back in the serial killer camp again?" I asked.

She nodded. "Listen. There are things I can't tell you about the investigation, things that aren't for the public. Sorry. But I can tell you I was wrong about the puncture marks on Belle's neck. The M.E. and forensics say they were definitely made by snake fangs, not a hypodermic. So we're looking for someone who's comfortable handling snakes."

"Anything on the hair or the buttons?"

"Lab says the hair came from a bunch of barber shops and salons, probably collected over a period of time."

"Premeditation."

"Yup. They haven't got much on the buttons, except they're not new."

"Killer thinks he's being funny," I remarked.

"How do you mean?"

"She was wearing a T-shirt, right? A T-shirt has no buttons. It's like that part in *Murder on the Orient Express* where Poirot says, 'too many clues.'"

"The murderer's trying to tell us something with the buttons, girl. All the profilers are sure of it."

"What is the psych profile on this, anyway?"

"Three different shrinks came up with three different answers." I raised my eyebrows in query, and she continued. "Randolph thinks we're dealing with a traditional serial killer, one with a snake fetish. Thinks the victims will all be women, but not necessarily lesbians. According to him, every scene will have a snake rattle—maybe in her pocket, maybe down her throat."

"Lovely."

"Ain't it?" She finished her coffee. "Anyway, Thackeray from the FBI did a quick consult for us. Based on photos of the crime scene he believes this is a hate crime; that lesbians are being specifically targeted by a man with feelings of inadequacy."

"That should narrow it down to thirty or forty million."

"My lieutenant agrees with Thackeray; that's why he's keeping me on the case. Otherwise, Homicide would take over. I'm working with them but right now, it's PC to assign me, just in case this is an anti-lesbian hate crime."

"What did the third shrink say?"

"The third is a forensic shrink on consult from L.A. She thinks the perp is convinced he or she loves Belle and was somehow doing her a favor by killing her. A stalker type, maybe. Killer convinces himself the victim reciprocates the relationship. She based her profile on how the victim was laid out; said the crime scene had 'veneration elements'."

"Did the three agree on anything?"

"Some. They all think the perp is most likely a white male in his thirties, maybe early forties. He's an organized thinker; plans things out. And they all agree the buttons are significant. You want my opinion, I think the profiles aren't worth spit."

"Do you ever get tired of dealing with ass wipes like Arlo George?" I asked.

"Occupational hazard of working hate crimes." Kari leaned back and stretched. "So, did you remember why Arlo George looked familiar?"

I averted my eyes. "Guess I was wrong about that."

She looked at me carefully. "You played me, Tess. Not cool. Not cool at all."

Frankly, I wasn't too proud of myself either. I took the fall-back position of righteous indignation. "Someone put a snake in my house, Kari. I want to know what the hell's going on."

In a tone revealing more than a little hurt, she said, "Well, you've just learned all you're gonna learn from me, girl. Get your butt outta here."

12

A TWIST
IN THE TO-DO LIST

I GREW UP ON A TINY ISLAND along the Jersey shore.
Back then, our beaches had no litter, no pollution, and no hu-
man debris—only vibrantly healing sand, wind, and ocean.
Horseshoe crabs, smelly and primeval. Pastel clamshells.
Moon snail sand collars. Necklaces of conch eggs drying in
the sun. Greenhead flies, iridescent eyes watching as they bit.
Jade salt water. Mud between your toes. It wasn't just a
beach; it was absolution from civilization.

On the bay side of the island grew marshlands full of
reeds and wild grasses. Thirty miles inland, south Jersey offered Pine Barrens, cranberry bogs, and cedar lakes. The one
thing we did not have, except on holiday weekends, was
crowds. Only then did the overflow from Atlantic City in-
undate our paradise.

Not only were San Diego beaches less pristine than those
of my childhood, but I also had to learn to share. In a metro-

politan area of two million souls, it's hard to find an empty strand.

One of the big bennies of my job at Imitech is a four-day work week with Wednesdays off. That's my play day, a day when I can lie on the beach without being conked by a swerving surfboard. I usually do chores and errands on Saturdays, and reserve Sundays for nature hikes and visits with friends. This Saturday I had the usual stops—dry cleaner, gym, and grocery store—but I'd added a twist to my to-do list. I was going to investigate Belle's murder.

I muscled through a sweaty workout at the gym—whining about the butt buster, as always—dropped two outfits at the cleaners, came home, showered, dressed, and launched my FX in the direction of Point Loma. A few minutes later, I pulled up in front of the Arlo George residence.

No way. Couldn't be. This meticulously maintained home with the brick trim and carefully sculpted landscaping simply couldn't belong to Arlo George, could it? Heavy drinkers with scrotums for frontal lobes don't do well enough in our society to afford houses like this. I double-checked the address I'd gotten from his police file. This was it, all right. No wonder lawyers were willing to dance to his tune. Even coming from someone in the larval stage of human growth, money talks.

As I walked to the front door, I reviewed my plan. I pressed the doorbell and smiled when a pleasant woman in her early sixties opened the door. "Good morning! I'm part of a neighborhood task force helping police canvas the area for tips regarding the woman who was murdered ten days ago." I held up an official-looking clipboard.

"I don't know anything about that, hon."

"Well, we want to cover all the bases. Sometimes you don't know how much you know." I barely refrained from adding, 'You know?' Humor in check, I continued. "We'd like to speak with all family members. Is everyone home right now?"

"It's just me and my husband; he'll be back this afternoon. If you want to come back then . . ."

"I'm afraid the task force has me assigned to another block this afternoon. If I could just have a few minutes of your time?"

"Come in." She opened the door and gestured toward a seat on her sofa.

Something about this was really wrong. I'd met wives of Arlo George types before—they had a joyless aspect to them and rarely looked you in the eye. This woman wore dark green linen slacks, a gold silk blouse, touches of gold jewelry, Italian leather shoes, and a clear, inquisitive look. I could see pain in her eyes but not devastation. I looked at my clipboard and asked, "Great. Let's get started. According to the municipal records, this is the primary residence of Arlo and Virginia George?"

She nodded. "My husband and I own this property."

"As I'm sure you know from the media coverage, the victim lived only a few blocks from your home. Did you or your husband know her?"

A slight but definite hesitation. "I didn't recognize her from the pictures in the news. I can't speak for Arlo." She picked her words like kids pick wild blackberries from stickery vines: very, very carefully. "I was having tea; can I get you something to drink?"

"No thanks, this won't take long. Just a few more questions." I pretended to consult the clipboard again. "Were you and your husband in the neighborhood the day of the murder? You might have seen something that would help identify a suspect."

Mrs. George relaxed into the sofa and recollected. While she thought, I observed. Good furniture, well polished. No stains. Luscious gray Berber carpet. On the fireplace mantle, a wedding portrait of her and Arlo. Arlo stood sober, tan, and bright eyed in a dress Merchant Marine uniform, a protective hand on the shoulder of his bride. The features were Arlo's but the sense of promise was completely different from the grunge I'd seen at the police station yesterday. The bride in the photo looked naïve, infatuated, and plump. Pregnant plump.

My hostess finally went to the dining room, opened a buffet drawer, and pulled out some paperwork. She returned and handed it to me, nodding. "That's what I thought. Arlo was out of town at the time of the murder."

I examined the flyer for the IMO Solid Cargo and Containers Conference. The section you send in for reservations had been removed. The dates matched. If Arlo attended, he was out of town when Belle Farby was killed. Damn.

I realized Mrs. George was talking to me. ". . . so I had to leave a message with the hotel switchboard. He called me back a few hours later. See, the plumber we'd used for years retired and this new one gave me such a high estimate. I wanted to check with Arlo before I gave him the work."

I stood up to go. "And you don't remember seeing anybody or anything strange around the neighborhood the day of the murder?"

"Not that I recall."

I drifted toward the wedding portrait and looked at it carefully. The photographer had touched up the color of Arlo's eyes so they almost matched each other. "Having a husband in the Merchant Marines can't be easy. You must've been alone much of the time."

"Separation can be good for a marriage." Her body language steered me to the front door.

"Thanks for your help," I said as I clipped down her front steps.

Sitting in my car, I processed what I'd learned. A tiny Quasimodo rang a bell in my neocortex—the hunchback of hunches was ding-ing. This one would be easy enough to check out. If true, it might get me reinstated in Kari's good graces.

I decided I had enough time to take a detour on my way to the grocery store. I turned the ignition, punched an address into the GPS system, and read the directions. I checked the odometer and the clock. Clutch in; chest out; hi, ho, Silver, away!

13

FOR WHOM THE BELLE TOLD

"I WAS IN THE NEIGHBORHOOD; thought I'd stop by to pick up my jacket," I said when Darlene opened her front door exactly 1.2 miles and three minutes from Arlo George's house.

She motioned me in. Without looking at me directly she said, "I can't live here any more." Boxes, cardboard wardrobes, and plastic storage bins filled the living room. She wore dark blue Capri pants, an oversized blue oxford shirt, and sandals. She was braless—not that I noticed. Her hair was tied back with a blue and gold scarf printed with Horus, Ra, and Seth. I'd seen it on sale at the Museum Art Store last summer. Apparently the stereo wasn't yet boxed. From somewhere within, Sinatra was playing. I'm not a fan, but somehow for this atmosphere it worked.

Darlene returned to the floor amid cartons, packing tape, and strewn possessions. She pulled a bottle of Corona out from behind a box and took a swallow. "If you're thirsty, help yourself." She gestured toward the kitchen. "There's beer, Crystal Light, maybe milk. A few glasses are still in the cupboard over the sink."

I helped myself to a Corona, naked without the lime, and wondered why she wasn't going for my jacket. She looked at me.

"It's Tess, right?"

I nodded.

"Tell me again why you dropped by?" Her hands rested lightly on a box of dishtowels, candles, and rolled coins; her eyes, a bit unfocused, rested on me.

"For my jacket, and, uh, I also wanted to re-connect with you; talk about the murder. If we put our heads together without cop interference, we might come up with something."

"I think Sergeant Dixon is competent. I'm content to leave it to her."

Subtlety is not my forte, but there were undercurrents in the conversation even I couldn't miss. Darlene's body language was as seductive as a pair of stiletto heels. Her words said go away, leave it to the police. Her body said 'unpack your bag and put your toothbrush in the bathroom.' Or did it?

"Well, even if the detective is capable, don't you think she deserves all the help she can get? You want to see whoever killed Belle go to prison, don't you?"

"To be honest, Tess . . ." A teasing hiss on the *s* . . . "What difference does it make? Whoever killed her, she's gone. Gone. That's all that matters."

"Look, if you really don't want to talk, I'll take my jacket and go."

The word 'jacket' seemed to snap her back into pragmatic nurse mode, the side of her that dealt successfully with veins and stitches, bedpans and serum.

"Your jacket, yes. I think it's in the bedroom. 'Scuse me." She walked toward the rear of the condo.

I explored the remaining shell of a living room. Must be my day to snoop family mementos. In one open box a yearbook from some small town in Tennessee peeked out along with several Roy Orbison records, and a bowling trophy. In another box, photos in albums and frames reflected images of happier times. The top picture in the box, a framed color 5 x 7, showed Belle at a lakeside picnic with some of the folks I'd seen at the cemetery. I was studying it when Darlene returned.

"You were at the memorial service, weren't you?" she asked.

"Sergeant Dixon asked me to attend. I think some of these people were there, too."

She tossed my jacket on a carton near the front door and came over to where I stood. "Old friends, mostly from her navy days."

"Navy chiefs and lesbians—a colorful combo. Is that why you didn't have a chaplain or minister at the service?"

"The church I was raised in was too fanatical for my comfort. I left it when I was seventeen and never looked back. And Belle was agnostic. A religious service wasn't important."

She seemed receptive to questions, so I pushed on to more sensitive matters. "Who's Belle's beneficiary?"

"She left her share of our house to Mamma's Kitchen."
Mamma's Kitchen is a local charity that feeds the body and
spirit of AIDS victims. Darlene continued. "That's another
reason I need to move. They'll want to sell the house; cash is
more useful to them. She left her grandnephew a small savings account. I'm beneficiary of her life insurance. I'll have
enough to buy a small place of my own."

"Had Belle told anyone else the contents of her will?" I
asked.

"Don't know; don't think I ever asked Belle that."

"What about her ex-husband? Were they on friendly
terms? I didn't see him at the service."

"He pulled a Richard Corey years ago."

"How did he do it?"

"Hanged himself in their bedroom closet. The marriage
wasn't working; she'd filed for divorce. He never protested.
They were still living together, platonically, while she looked
for a place of her own. Then one day she came home, and
there he was." An odd smile turned one side of her lip. "It's
what got Belle out of her own closet." Darlene relocated her
Corona, took a long sip, and sank onto a floor pillow. "She
saw how truly miserable his life had been—*their* lives had
been. She was afraid she'd end up like him if she didn't make
some drastic changes." Darlene sealed a box with packing
tape. "Three months after he died, she joined the navy, and
came out to her friends as a lesbian."

I could feel myself distancing from this sad, secretive
soap opera. Melodrama belongs on stage; a lump in my breast
was melodramatic enough, thank you. I tuned her out and
entertained a rather satisfying, though brief, sexual fantasy,
which gave me the distance I needed to re-enter the conversa-

tion. When it comes to all this touchy-feely take-your-inner-child-for-a-bike-ride stuff, I still need training wheels.

I poured cool beer down my throat. Damn, I really missed the lime. I changed the subject. "The newspaper said Belle was originally from Oregon?"

Darlene nodded.

"Then you must be the one from Tennessee." I indicated the yearbook in the other box.

Darlene seemed to gather herself. "So what?"

"Well, if Belle was in Oregon and you were in Tennessee, how did the two of you meet?"

"When we met she'd already left Oregon and joined the navy. They hire civilians at military hospitals; I was working at NAS Memphis Medical Center. Belle came in for an appendectomy."

Maybe that's why I hadn't met the love of my life: I still have my appendix. Tonsils, too, for that matter. "Did Belle mention any trouble she was in? Was anything worrying her?"

"Tess," same slight sibilance on the *s*, "Belle didn't talk much about herself. She barbecued steaks. She paid bills. She spoon-fed her father during his last days. She wore the same clothes a lot. She watched the same TV shows week after week." Darlene swallowed hard. "She took out the trash. She took me fishing; she checked the air pressure in our tires. She was steadfast and sweet and a hard worker . . ." Her voice caught. "Belle loved domesticity. She was happy . . . *We* were happy." Darlene swallowed more tears. "This place feels so empty. I can't sleep at night."

I bent down where she was sitting, put my hand on her shoulder, and asked, "Should I call someone to come stay with you?" She shook her head no. I tried to comfort her. "The hymn you sang at her service—that was awesome. I'm sure Belle appreciated it, wherever she is."

She managed half a smile, stood up slowly, and at last handed me my jacket. "You'd better go now."

As I pulled away from the curb, it occurred to me that the slight slur of words and friendly body language probably stemmed from one too many Coronas. She hadn't been expecting company and she'd probably put away several before I got there. There are times when the most mature of us need pacifiers.

14

PRO BONO
NO LOGO

LIKE DARLENE, I HAD NO DATE this Saturday night. Waiting for the mammo results caused Mexican jumping beans to cavort in my nerve centers. I asked Lana for a back massage, but she said she'd already done too many massages that week, and left to attend a holistic health lecture with friends.

To distract myself, I began brainstorming on Belle's case. Recalling the hunch I had after talking to Virginia George, I went to my room and logged on the Internet. Google and I searched for and found the International Maritime Organization. I checked their Web site, did another search, then spent eight minutes on the phone with a representative from a dot com.

Smug with self-satisfaction, I called Kari on her personal cell. I wasn't sure of her work schedule, but even on a Saturday, I felt sure she'd want to hear my revelation. "Kari, it's Tess."

"Yeah, what's up?"

"I feel bad about the other day, and thought maybe some new information might make up for it," I ventured.

"I'm pissed at you, girl. You used me. You're not gonna gloss over this one."

"OK, OK. I'm not glossing, I'm sharing information. Arlo George wasn't at the IMO convention in San Francisco when Belle was killed."

"Whatcha got?" I heard something besides anger in her tone—curiosity.

"The other day George made a big point of telling us that his wife called him while he was in 'Frisco. That sounded defensive. It reminded me of a magazine article I read about companies that sell alibis, mainly to adulterous husbands. For a fee the company prints up dummy flyers or brochures for fake conventions and meetings, and provides a phone number that serves as a phony switchboard. The staffers who answer that number will get messages to you, wherever you really are, so you can call back your wife or your boss."

"I've heard about those outfits. Go on."

"Virginia George showed me Arlo's brochure for the convention. It didn't have IMO's logo printed on it anywhere. What organization sends out flyers without their logo? I hit pay dirt with youralibi.com; they're up in L.A. Told them I was with the police and they confirmed Arlo George was a customer."

Instead of being pleased, Kari took serious offense at this and hung up on me.

I dialed her right back. "What's with you? Not enough fiber in your diet? I thought you'd be happy to get a viable suspect with a fake alibi. I was trying to make it up to—"

She cut me off. "You don't have a friggin' clue, do you? First off, Arlo George isn't a viable suspect. His alibi might be fake—which we would have found out on our own, thank you very much—but his back injury isn't. His spine's made of Rice Krispees; no way could he be hauling any bodies around. Besides, he doesn't fit any of the profiles."

"Oh," was all I could get out of my very deflated self.

"Girl, I got work to do with some real suspects. I know you were only tryin' to help, so I'm not gonna fry you for interfering with an ongoing police investigation or impersonating an officer. But do me a favor and leave this to us, OK?"

It was pretty clear that whether I agreed or not, Kari was not open to further suggestions. "Look, if I promise not to interfere, will you answer just one question for me?"

"Depends. What is it?"

"Do they know what poison killed Belle?"

"I tell you, then you're out of my face, right?"

"Right."

"Well, it'll be in tomorrow's newspapers anyway. It was a snake venom. But not rattlesnake. Some Australian snake; can't remember the name now, but it's just about the most toxic venom going. And yes, we're talking to people at the zoo. I gotta go."

"Good luck." I hung up. Arlo George hadn't been the most promising suspect. I tended to believe his statement about fearing snakes. You could get elected president if you had a vote from each person with an aversion to snakes and you wouldn't need the Supreme Court to do it.

That night I dreamt I was on the island of Chincoteague. Dank salt breeze blew in off the ocean. I ambled over white sand dunes up into a marshy field where spotted ponies munched grass and swatted flies with their tails. Puffy clouds daubed the sky. In my peripheral vision, I glimpsed movement. I turned and saw a spidery orange crab crawling up from the shore toward the field. I figured he must be lost. But soon more and more crabs came—twenty, sixty, hundreds. They made the ponies nervous. The crabs grew bigger and closed in on the horses and me. I turned to escape, but they had multiplied so quickly, there was nowhere to run.

15

ME AND
TOM HANKS

I was marooned on an island; around me seas roiled. Wind battered all shelter; branches cracked and crashed.

My island was an examining table in the office of Dr. Margot Winter, the surgeon most experienced with mastectomies and breast cancer in my medical group. She was an intense woman in her late thirties. Her face bore a few acne scars and she smelled of Betadine yet she was otherwise quite attractive.

My island was lonely and cold; my body exposed except for a paper gown. I shivered. How did I get here? When did my ship wreck?

Dr. Winter was telling me she needed a biopsy to confirm that my tumor was malignant, then she could schedule surgery. My enthusiasm for a biopsy wouldn't fill a triple-A cup.

A biopsy meant a needle—a big mother of a needle—and

I have a phobia about needles. Not an aversion, not a fear. A full-blown phobia. I'm OK with spiders, heights, flying, even snakes, but in movies when they show an addict shooting up, I have to turn my head or I'll pass out. I postponed the blood test for my marriage license so long that Roark and I had only ten minutes to get the test results to the magistrate's office before they closed, the day before the wedding. A phobia.

I explained my problem to Dr. Winter. "So I'd rather decline the biopsy."

She didn't get it. "I can't operate on you without a biopsy. That would be insane."

"Why?" I asked from behind a thrashed island palm.

"We have to be *sure*."

"My primary care doc is sure. When you examined my breast, you looked pretty sure."

Dr. Winter furrowed her brow and smacked my medical chart down on a counter. She was a driven woman with no time for uncooperative patients. She raised her voice. The skies above my island darkened. "Look, it's just not done. We cannot do surgery on you without being certain. I'd be leaving myself open to a potential malpractice suit."

"If I decide not to have the mastectomy, how long do I have?"

Dr. Winter looked in my eyes, exasperation muted by compassion. "It's a large tumor. Maybe six months."

Six months? Criminitlies! I feel great. I feel fine. I have no pain. This can't be real; I must be in a movie. I'm marooned on this island and a voice in the wind is telling me I have to do something I can't do or I'll die in six months. There must be some way around this clinical Chinese wall. "Can you anesthetize me with a gas mask and then do the biopsy?"

"We use a local anesthetic, Lidocaine."

I felt at one with Tom Hanks in *Castaway*, subject to the ravages of nature. "I can't have you poking my breast with a gigantic needle while I'm awake. I'll hyperventilate. I'll puke. I just can't do it."

Dr. Winter picked up my mammogram films, held them to the light box, and scrutinized. She did some controlled breathing. If I'd had hatches, I'd have battened them. "We need to get you a surgery date as soon as possible. I'll waive the biopsy."

Although I was still marooned on the table, a ray of sun shone down on me. "Thank you. Really, thank you. Um . . . what do I do now?"

"Here are the names of some specialists—a plastic surgeon, an oncologist, and a radiologist." She handed me the business cards of three physicians. "Make appointments with each of them as soon as possible. I'll see you back in two weeks."

"I have a question."

"What is it?"

"Do you think faith alone could heal this tumor?"

Immediately, firmly: "No. Faith alone will put you in a coffin. And I believe in God. I pray before every surgery."

Somehow I liked her better for that. The storm front cleared. I dressed and left the island, taking my advanced tumor with me.

16

GOT SWIZZLE?

After the appointment I was too *varmisht* to go back to the office so I went home. Lana was out at one of her myriad non-reportable income venues. I picked out a homemade CD of nineties pop rock that usually cheers me up and put it in the stereo. I paced from my bedroom to the living room, kitchen, and sunporch with the CD blasting. Dishwalla sang, "Tell me all your thoughts on God, 'cause I'm on my way to meet Her." I sang along and trailed tears and self-pity through the house. I was on my way to meet Her thirty-five years too soon. Raj, tense and vigilant, stayed close.

By the time the Dave Matthews Band suggested, "Hike up your skirt a little more and show your world to me," I felt considerably better, whether from the catharsis of tears or the conjured image, I'm not sure. I responded to e-mails from Celeste and Tiger and printed more info from Roark.

His e-mails indicated that SDPD had called Darlene Nealson in for questioning again, gaining no helpful information. The file contained her new address. She now lived on the other side of my neighborhood, Mission Hills, about two miles from my place.

I poured myself a Tanqueray gin on the rocks. Wish I had swizzle sticks; I could use a little swizzle in my life right now.

Over breakfast this morning, I'd told Lana about the crab dream. She said in astrology, the crab is the symbol for cancer. Cancer, duh. I don't believe in astrology, but apparently my subconscious does.

I retrieved the cards Dr. Winter had given me for the three specialists. My insurance entitled me to breast reconstruction, so I understood why a plastic surgeon was involved. But an oncologist? Their thing is chemo—administered by an IV needle. Chemo would need success statistics as impressive as Wonder Woman's bust line for it to be worth the trauma, to me. And the radiologist? X-ray techs wear lead aprons for a reason. I needed to research both treatments before my appointments.

A quick topic search on the Internet showed me that chemo cures cancer. And Essaic tea cures cancer. Bioresonance, water therapy, and laetrile cure cancer. Shark cartilage cures cancer. Only cartilage from wheat grass-drinking sharks cures cancer. Yet cancer kills so very many. Opinions were plentiful but I needed to know which books contained objective data based on legitimate studies. Darlene was a nurse; she might know which resources could be trusted. Maybe I could combine my murder investigation with personal business.

I decided to walk to Darlene's; the exercise would do me good. The streets of Mission Hills are lined with well tended Craftsman and Spanish-style homes landscaped with palms and pine, bird-of-paradise and bougainvillea, hibiscus and honeysuckle. In the area where Darlene now lived, the streets thread up and down through canyons. After two steep uphill stints, my legs were whining like spoiled kids on a long drive. At the crest of the last hill, I stopped to watch as a mauve and marigold sunset splashed jubilance over San Diego harbor.

Darlene's house was a humble white stucco with a red tile roof and bougainvillea crawling to the eaves. Her Subaru was parked out front. I climbed her front porch. The wooden inside door was halfway open but there were no lights on inside. I called through the screen door. "Darlene? It's Tess Camillo."

No water running in the bath or shower. No caps popping off Coronas. No clack of sandals from one room to the next. No TV droning. No vibrator buzzing. But I did hear something: low groans, movement. And the unmistakable sound of a person retching.

"Darlene! It's Tess. Are you OK?"

The movements and moans continued. The screen door was unlocked. I let myself in. I flicked on a light switch and glanced around the living room past half-unpacked boxes. I checked the kitchen. Nobody there. I found the hall light and switched it on. Cautiously I crept down the hall toward the noises. The first door on my right was shut. I opened it and almost immediately a rattlesnake slithered from the room into the hallway.

The snake crept into a bathroom farther down the hall. I promptly closed the door behind it, securing the varmint, I hoped.

I entered the room where the snake had been. Writhing on the floor in her own vomit, doubled over with pain, lay

Darlene Nealson. Her breathing was labored and she was sweating profusely. One of her ankles was bleeding.

I called 911. This time no one gave me any crap about letting Animal Control handle it.

17

SEVEN CARS
FROM JERSEY

You never do anything inane, right? Never swallow your gum? Punch the wrong hole on a butterfly ballot? Rub against wet paint? Make paper clip chains? Me neither. Yet on my way to the hospital during lunch hour the next day I counted Jersey license plates. In the heavy traffic of my nineteen-minute drive, the tally came to seven, a lucky number. If snakebites were anything like craps, maybe Darlene would be OK.

She must've had seven doctors, seven nurses, and seven vials of antivenin. She was sitting up in bed watching TV. Other than an ice pack on her raised ankle, she looked pretty damned good. "Hi," she said as she clicked off CNN. Her hazel eyes took me in. "I hear you rescued me."

"I'll return for your firstborn child later," I teased. I had my hands full. I set my car keys and purse down along with the bouquet of pink and yellow carnations wrapped in green florist paper. I looked around the room for an empty vase. No luck. "I'll be right back." I zipped out to the nearest nurses' station, scrounged a vase from them, filled it with water in the ladies' room, and arranged the carnations as well as I could. I'm no Mies van der Rohe but at least they looked cheerful. Good thing, because Darlene seemed depressed. "There was this viper who was truly poverty stricken—he didn't have a pit to hiss in."

Darlene grimaced. I didn't blame her, but it was the best I could do for snake jokes on short notice. "Are you as recovered as you look?" I asked, trying again for a positive note.

"I might be released later today. The sooner, the better." Her tone was flat. She adjusted the pillow behind her back. "We nurses make the worst patients."

"I thought rattlesnake bites were pretty serious?"

"It depends on how much venom the snake injects. I must have a guardian angel because the one that bit me didn't inject a full load of venom." She shrugged at the strangeness of it all.

"What exactly happened?"

"I was off yesterday. In the morning I went grocery shopping. Came home, unpacked a few boxes, ate lunch, and took a nap. When I woke up, I did more unpacking. Around 5:30, I heard a knock at the front door. My friend, Laura, was coming for dinner at 6:30. I thought she got her signals crossed and came early, so I opened the door without thinking."

I'd seen a woman arrive at Darlene's just as the ambulance was pulling away. Must've been Laura.

She continued. "This guy was standing there with his hand inside his jacket. The screen wasn't locked. He barged in. Then he pulled his hand out of the jacket and shoved the damn snake right at me." Darlene's mouth was a changeling, moving from the doorstep of depression to the foyer of fury. "I backed away as fast as I could and he chased me down the hall. I ran into the front bedroom. He threw the snake into the room with me and held the door shut. I figured I'd escape through the window but I tripped on something and fell. I remember seeing the snake near my ankle. That's about all I remember." Darlene sipped from a water glass on her night-stand. "No, I take that back. I also have fond memories of vomiting."

"Well, at least you can give the police a description of the man."

"A *general* description, yes. He was white, probably in his thirties, maybe five-eight. He wore a ball cap pulled down over his face, so I didn't get a good look at his features or hair. As you can imagine," she added dryly, "my attention was on the snake."

"Did you recognize his voice? His body language?"

She laughed without amusement. "You're a real Miss Marple. The police asked me the same thing this morning when they took my statement. The guy never said a word, so I didn't hear his voice. I have no idea who he was."

"Well, I'm glad you're OK. Your statement will probably help in the investigation."

"Maybe."

She seemed so down; perhaps it was medication? "Darlene, is there something else? Something I can help you with maybe?"

Those hazel eyes grew tearful. The words choked out, clogged with sniffles and raw hurt. "It just seems so . . . After thirty years Belle was like a part of me, like my hands, my eyes. Going on with life without her is, I don't know, unnatural, almost." She grabbed a tissue and made good use of it. In doing so, she bumped the vase of flowers I'd brought her, but caught them before they tipped over. "I didn't even thank you for these. That was nice of you."

"How about if I move them to the window ledge? That way you can see them without turning your head." I matched the action to the words and she nodded in appreciation.

"Actually," I began, "I came over to your house yesterday evening to ask you something."

Something in her eyes closed down. "Tess, if you're on the make, I'm sorry, not interested." She pushed a reddish curl from her brow. "I don't know if there'll ever be anybody else."

"It's nothing like that. It's just that I'm going to be in a hospital bed soon and . . ." I explained my diagnosis and consequent need for reliable medical resources. She perked up a bit; I tried not to take it personally.

She sat up a little straighter in bed. "As far as the Internet goes, the best place to start is . . ." She gave me the URL for the informative Web site of a woman M.D. breast cancer specialist that lists many resources. "Also, the American Cancer Society and the National Cancer Institute have statistics on the success of different treatments, if that's what you're looking for."

I grabbed my PDA and entered the information. "What about books?" I asked.

"The nursing supervisor in Cardio had breast cancer last year. She recommended . . ."

I noted the titles. "If I have more questions later, do you mind if I contact you?"

"Feel free. My cell number is 619-555-9791. You know, no matter how scared you are of needles, you really should get that biopsy."

At the mention of a word beginning with "n" and ending in "eedle," I decided our visit was over. A glance at my watch showed I had eight and a half minutes to drive fourteen miles to get back to work on time. I thanked Darlene and sped my Silver Bullet into the freeway fray where I imagined cars with What Would Ellen Do? bumper stickers.

18

A PAIR OF QUEENS

To my right sat Jiminy Cricket; around me, a Tours4You bus driver, and a pirate. It was October 31, the M&M's were nearly gone, and the kids had stopped knocking. Every few months, Lana and I gather our closest friends for a poker night; we were into our second hand of the evening. Two of us chomped bubble gum cigars to avoid the temptation of leftover candy.

Lana sat on my left, munching broccoli dipped in hummus. I couldn't quite figure out her costume: small white wings affixed to a karate gi, black tights, and duck feet bedroom slippers. A wounded seagull? The kung fu fairy?

Tiger, a.k.a. Titania Ford, a sprite with auburn hair, green eyes, quick wit, and Irish brooding, dealt one more down and dirty. Tiger works as production manager at a local theater, indulging her passion for props while falling in love with a series of highly unsuitable actors. Tonight she wore a buccaneer outfit on loan from a show.

Lana's friend, Trang Nguyen, and my pal, Celeste Moss, rounded out the group.

"I've got some news," I announced. "I've also got a pair of queens." I showed the cards and drew the pot of chips toward me. I looked around the poker circle and took a deep breath. "A few weeks ago, I discovered a lump in my left breast." Suddenly you could hear a one-eyed jack blink. Through a tightening throat, I formed the words. "I have breast cancer; lobular invasive carcinoma. A big tumor."

Tiger reached over and took my hand. I felt strangely detached, like we were talking about a neighbor's battle with crabgrass. "Sorry about dropping this bomb on you tonight, but you're all here now and I don't want to have to repeat this over and over." I didn't tell them I feared the authority of the words. How many times can you declare, "I have cancer" to others without endowing that phrase with power?

Tiger was a long-faced Long Jane Silver. Trang seemed in shock. Jiminy Cricket, otherwise known as Celeste Moss, turned toward me. A few years younger than most of us and the only one who was married, Celeste has a mind that grasps metaphysics as readily as geophysics. She also has eyebrows that never need plucking. She probably regulates their growth through meditation; wouldn't surprise me. She runs the local noetic sciences think tank and talks over my head so often I should bring a stepladder to our visits. Celeste promised, "I'll send you orange energy every day."

Trang asked, "I thought you got regular mammograms?"

"I do. I had one last February. My doctor says this lobular kind of breast cancer is hard to detect on mammos until the advanced stages."

"What're you going to do?" This from Tiger.

"The tumor is advanced. I'll need a mastectomy." Gasps came from several directions.

"Chemo and radiation?" Trang wondered.

"So far my research shows chemo helps a lot when aggressive breast cancer tumors are caught early, but for big tumors its effectiveness is ambiguous. And the radiologist said he couldn't zap my chest wall without collateral damage to my heart and lung cells. I've been in the military; collateral damage is something you try hard to avoid, especially when it involves organs that keep you alive. So, I think I'll opt out of chemo and radiation. I'll check alternative therapies. If the cancer has spread to my lymph nodes, I'm gonna need more than pixie dust."

For the next few minutes I drowned in questions and encouragement. I appreciated all of it, but it grew too intense. "OK, Trang's deal. What'll it be?"

The thirty-something Vietnamese beauty thought for a moment. "Five card stud, deuces wild."

We anted and soon were back in a game. Everyone tried to ignore the elephant in the corner, but a breast cancer diagnosis is a real Jumbo. A distraction would help.

"I'll bet ten." I threw a chip into the pot. "Hey, did I tell you I'm conducting my very own murder investigation?"

I caught them up on events of the Belle Farby case. Lana, who already knew the saga, refilled a bowl with pretzels and refreshed drinks. Probably peeked at cards, too.

"You're bluffing," Tiger told Celeste after she upped the bid. "I'll see you and raise you five." Chips clinked; pretzels crunched.

I scanned the table under my feet and found Raj. "Hey, buddy," I said, showing him my cards. "What do you think?

Hold or fold?" Raj licked my fingers three times rapidly, which I interpreted as a recommendation to hold.

"Was Roark able to send you anything?" asked Celeste.

"It's amazing what he got his hands on. He sent all the police reports on the case, plus some background information. A couple files got corrupted in transmission but I could tell from the file names they were just the Arlo George interview and the coroner's report. I already knew about them."

"What did you find out?" Trang chimed in as she loosened the collar of her bus driver's uniform. She'd come right from work, but her uniform served well as Halloween garb. On me, the uniform would've looked butch; on Trang, it had Dietrich–in-a-tux appeal.

"Well, the police ran the case through the national crime database; no other murders have been reported anywhere with this hair/buttons/snake M.O. They also checked the Union Bank angle—no employees work at both Hillcrest and Point Loma branches. Darlene took one extension course at UCSD a while ago, but neither Belle nor Darlene had any other connection to the university. Police interviewed friends and neighbors, scrutinized three months of phone records, came up with—" I gave Tiger a nod, "—much ado about nothing.' They even questioned the hospice aide who helped out when Belle's father was dying."

Celeste joked, "No ex-snake charmers, huh?"

"Not even a pet boa. What the police discovered was that Belle and Darlene were a lavender Ozzie and Harriet."

Lana won the hand and counted her chips. She picked up a chip and stared at it. "Do you think the colors of the American flag came from poker chips?"

That one silenced us until Celeste steered us back to the subject. "What about the buttons, Tess? Any more on that?"

"Not a thing, except the profilers still think they're significant."

"The hairs alone show that Darlene didn't do it," Trang offered. "If Darlene killed Belle, she wouldn't be paranoid about hairs found on Belle's clothing. They'd *expect* her hair to be on Belle's clothes; they lived together. But if someone else killed Belle, then sprinkling hairs all over makes sense. The cops don't know which hairs are significant."

"That was my take, too." I finished dealing. "Let's do a round of Spit in the Ocean."

"Gotta love that name," remarked Tiger.

"Tess likes anything related to tongues and mouths!" joked Trang.

"You got no room to talk, woman. Every time you deal, it's 'stud' this, and 'stud' that," I teased back. "Anyway, the cops have two primary suspects . . ."

"Let's hear it!" they urged.

The distraction was working. I began the data dump. "First there's Mr. Wade 'Mongoose' Matthews, a white supremacist, thirty-eight; lives alone out in Borrego Desert. He was arrested ten years ago for a rape that took place . . ." My fingers did a little drum roll on the table, ". . . near the UCSD library—about thirty feet from the Snake Path. He got off on a technicality. Guess how he makes a living? He milks rattlers and sells the venom to antivenin labs."

"He's guilty!" Trang declared. "They should throw his butt in jail right now!"

"Much as I'd love to see a white supremacist in prison, he's got an alibi. He was in Julian the day Belle was murdered. He's got receipts from a couple stores he visited, and his dentist did the prep work for two crowns that day." Interest in poker was dwindling; murder held more intrigue. I folded, and everyone else soon followed.

"The cops will break his alibi. He did it," Trang insisted.

"Who else is in the running?" Celeste was interested.

"The zoo put the cops on to the only other viable suspect—a herpetologist named Susan Duffy."

"I know her!" said Tiger. "She was my neighbor until just a few months ago, when I moved to Encinitas. Her ghost light's on, but no one's home."

"How so?" I asked.

"Sometimes she'd just stand out on her patio holding a pet iguana and stare up at the sky for twenty, thirty minutes, like she was waiting for Scottie to beam her up. She had a good job with the zoo, but she just up and quit one day. People wait years to get decent jobs at the zoo."

"Is she married?" Tiger might have more info on her private life than the police.

"She's bi. Got a boyfriend who's almost as weird as she is—Sean, or John something, I think. Saw him with her once." Tiger took a sip of her Irish whiskey on the rocks, which enhanced her pirate demeanor. "Just before I moved, she asked me if I knew any single lesbians I could hook her up with. Don't worry; I never mentioned you, Tess."

"Dodged a bullet, did I?" I got up and disposed of my bubble gum, circumventing Pookie on my way back to the table. "Remember anything else about her?"

Tiger shook her head. "I wondered if she had mental problems. I wasn't mean to her, but I wasn't exactly motivated to get close. Last I heard she was going to put a personal ad online."

"Did she know Belle or Darlene?" Trang asked.

"Not according to her police statement, but who knows?"

Minutes after midnight, our guests were leaving. Celeste twirled her Jiminy Cricket umbrella and said, "I have an odd sense about this Belle Farby murder, Tess. There's more to this than meets the eye. A psychic or spiritual aspect, maybe. Be careful."

"You know I'm not into that woo woo stuff, Celeste," I replied, "but I appreciate your concern. I'll keep an eye out." I hugged her good-bye.

When our guests had gone Lana and I did a little KP, and then headed down the hall to our respective rooms. I stopped her. "I gotta know: what's your costume supposed to be?"

She laughed. "I'm the Ugly Duckling. When I wake up tomorrow, I'll be a beautiful swan. 'Night."

Funny, her smile alone had always made her swan enough for me.

19

THE REVOLUTION

The week before my surgery wasn't the most ecstatic. I heard a TV commercial for tampons with the tag line, "The Revolution Continues." Apparently I was part of that revolution: the government of my uterus was being taken over by a cadre of cramps. I mixed myself a martini that could do push-ups.

Lana came home from registering for a community college class. She took one look at me and said, "Sorry you're not feeling well."

"Just started what has all the signs of a really crappy period. But how did you know?" She just smiled. After a long sip of martini, I turned to get more ice from the fridge and tripped over Pookie. Damn! That dog has all the charm of a hemorrhoid. Once my drink was freshened, I continued, "I told the folks at the office about the tumor. They were really decent. Melissa's getting the disability paperwork processed."

"Glad you've got their support." Lana held up a colorful text. "I got that Southwest Native American Culture class I wanted!" In California's overloaded community college system, it's a crapshoot whether you'll get the classes you want before your ninety-second birthday.

After dinner I holed up in my room. I was just out of sorts enough to realize I'd kick Pookie to Peoria if she got under my feet again. I didn't even let Raj in. Figured it might be good for all parties if I kept to my revolutionary self.

I booted up, logged on, and opened an awaiting message from Roark. Updated info slid down the cyber-banister. The FBI informed SDPD that Mongoose Matthews had once been the target of an FBI investigation. He and his white supremacist buddies were suspected of putting snake skins in the mailboxes of prominent Hispanics, blacks, and Jews to intimidate them. Yup, snake skins. It sucks that this guy had an alibi.

Roark had also retransmitted the two files that corrupted the first time: the SDPD interview with Arlo George and the autopsy report. Minus the spilled Pepsi, the George interview accurately recorded what I remembered. According to the latest reports, SDPD had essentially abandoned the idea of a hate crime or serial killer and were focused on who had issues with the Darlene/Belle household. The post-mortem report reminded me of how unique every human body is: Belle's left leg was 1/8-inch shorter than the right; one ventricle in her brain was more spacious than most people's; she had a strawberry birthmark directly under the fang marks on her neck; and her nasal septum was deviated. She was unique all right—murdered and uniquely dead. Control of the case was transitioning from Hate Crime Liaison Sergeant Kari Dixon to a regular homicide detective.

The police were making new inquiries but had no new leads. Rattler Man left no physical evidence they could differentiate. Darlene's new home had been up for sale for months before she bought it. Many potential buyers had come through; there were too many fingerprints and fibers for any of them to be useful. There were no shoe prints, no blood other than Darlene's. Da nada. Could you dust a snake for fingerprints?

SDPD had not honed in on either of the suspects: Mongoose Matthews still lacked the opportunity, due to his dentist appointment alibi; Susan Duffy still lacked any apparent motive. Roark also mentioned he'd be leaving for a long vacation. He and an Old Spice type would soon be touring Tuscany.

I searched a couple of personals sites and found Susan Duffy's ad on Planet Out. She'd posted a photo that resembled the snapshots in the police file. The writer of that ad described herself as a reptile lover, an uncommon dating gambit. I was pretty sure I had the right woman. I responded to the ad and asked to meet at a coffeehouse. I might be able to learn more from the perspective of a date than police learned from the perspective of interrogators. Later I could brainstorm ways to question Mongoose Matthews.

She must've been online, too, because she quickly shot back a response confirming our rendezvous. I pulled up her personal ad again. Height? Five foot seven. Close enough to Darlene's estimate of Rattler Man at five foot eight. I looked at her build in the photo—small breasted, big boned. In men's clothing she could have pulled it off.

My bedroom door was open and Lana popped her head in. "Tess, have you seen the turquoise skirt I got in Santa Fe?

Nate's in town for a few days and I want to wear it when I see him."

Neither her ability to misplace items on a routine basis nor her lust for Nate came as a surprise. The thirty-one-year-old British soccer pro is ruggedly handsome, energetic, flirtatious, and he prefers older women. He likes Lana. Lana likes him. It was purely physical; there was little between them except pearls of semen on the sheets.

After assuring Lana I'd keep an eye out for her skirt, I soaked in a long hot bath with neroli and sandalwood oils, and went to bed.

I dreamt I was lying on my back bound to a four-poster bed. Woman after woman bent over me. I couldn't make out their features. Each woman maneuvered her breasts toward my mouth. Nipples came to within a sixteenth of an inch of my lips but I couldn't quite reach them.

Was I dreaming about breasts because of my diagnosis, or because Lana can still ice my Oreos? Where's Jung when you need him?

20

OXYURANUS

Susan Duffy reminded me of the roommate I was assigned during my first semester at Everette Bible Institute. Her name was Marge. Marge grew up in rural Wisconsin a few miles from Ed Gein's turf. She was socially backward even by Bible school standards, which was saying something.

She didn't shampoo often enough, she suffered from acne, and she went to bed by nine o'clock every night. She never had a date. She never missed a class. She studied hard. Every single night she got down on her knees beside her metal bunk bed and prayed aloud for her family and those she believed were her friends. She prayed for the sick. She prayed for the poor. She prayed for the unsaved. She prayed with sincerity so thick if it were syrup, you'd choke on it. She dropped out after one semester. Academically she only managed Ds and Fs, but she had more devotion than any professor I met there.

The soft overhead light of the Trolley Café on Park Boulevard reflected the shine from Susan Duffy's oily blonde hair. She had large blue eyes but her left eye muscle was weak, causing slightly skewed eye contact. She smelled musty. She fidgeted at first, but I soon found a way to put her at ease. All I had to do was talk snakes.

She hadn't found a new job yet, but she didn't seem bothered by the financial implications. Maybe she had money saved; maybe her parents helped support her. I asked her why she'd quit the zoo, but she talked around it. It wasn't difficult to transition from asking about her old job at the zoo to Belle's murder. "What kind of person would use a snake to kill someone?" I asked, keeping a close watch on her body language.

She sipped her blackberry tea and considered. "A snake is not a good murder weapon."

"Why not?"

"Snakes are living creatures, not objects you can fire like a gun. Lots of factors influence a snake to strike. You could go to all the trouble of obtaining a snake and getting the snake within striking distance of the intended victim and the snake might not perform his side of the deal." She scratched her head. I hoped nothing living emerged from under her fingernails. "On one hand, I'd say the murderer would have to be stupid to pick such an unreliable weapon. But they haven't caught the murderer yet, so maybe he's not so stupid."

Six young people entered the coffeehouse and huddled around the baked goods in the display counter. They laughed noisily and their multi-pierced faces seemed to intimidate Susan. I diverted her attention. The name of the snake whose venom killed Belle had been in the papers. Since it concerned snakes, I was sure Susan Duffy had read the article. "What can you tell me about this Australian snake, the one whose venom killed the woman?"

"*Oxyuranus microlepidotus.*" The words rolled off her tongue. "Otherwise known as the Inland Taipan or Fierce Snake. Most venomous land snake on the planet. The venom injected in a single bite can kill a hundred adults." Her eyes gleamed with Marge-like devotion.

"How would someone get one of these oxy-up-your-anus snakes?" I asked playfully.

"*Oxyuranus microlepidotus,*" she repeated carefully so I wouldn't get mixed up next time. "We have one at the zoo, but it was on display at the time that woman was murdered."

"Who else would have one?" I dipped a shortbread cookie into my cappuccino.

"Besides zoos? I'm sure there are private snake keepers with Inland Taipans but there's no way to check. There's no national or state registry of who owns what snakes. Most of them are kept discreetly and illegally. Except in Florida, where it used to be legal to own poisonous snakes. Maybe it still is. Then there are research centers. Lots of places are doing research with the toxins in venom."

"But research facilities are regulated by all kinds of watchdogs. Anyone getting a government grant has to file paperwork up the wazoo. You couldn't just snitch a snake from one of those places, could you?"

"Because government regulations are so complex, there's quite a black market for snakes. It's done even in reputable research centers, but nobody talks about it. It would be easy to get even less common snakes."

"But if a venomous snake disappeared from one of those places, they'd report it, right?"

"Not necessarily. No research facility wants the authorities scrutinizing how they run things."

"Any idea why the murderer would use that Oxy snake when there are plenty of rattlesnakes around?"

She shrugged. "If an *Oxyuranus microlepidotus* injected a full load of venom, it would certainly be the fastest kill."

In further conversation, Susan Duffy revealed that on the day Darlene was attacked, she had had a 10:00 A.M. job interview at the Los Angeles Zoo, then drove home. That would put her back in San Diego in plenty of time to disguise herself as Rattler Man.

We segued into dating topics: family, ex-lovers, and current hopes. She'd grown up on a farm in Missouri. Her grandparents raised her. Her mother died of cancer when she was six. She made no mention of her father. "What kind of cancer did your mother have?" I had to ask.

"Ovarian. Why?"

"Just wondered." I brought the evening to a close by swathing a bad news mummy in bandages of truth. "Susan, I'm not sure we have enough in common to date. You haven't mentioned it, but I've heard through the grapevine that you're bi. Is that true?"

"I guess so, if you have to use labels."

"I prefer not to become involved with women who still sleep with men. And I've got some health issues I just found out about that will take most of my time and energy. But I enjoyed talking to you. Thanks for coming." I stood up and held out my hand.

She smiled wanly and walked away.

Much later that night I sunk my head into my pillow. Shadows splotched the Saltillo tiles of my bedroom floor. I shut my eyes and thought about Celeste's eerie pronouncement on Halloween. A mystical or psychic aspect to Belle's murder? Hmm. Maybe I'll learn how to bend spoons with my thoughts. Maybe I'll regulate the growth of my eyebrows. Maybe I'll be able to grow a new breast.

Suddenly a shrill alarm signal speared my frontal lobe, accompanied by the yammering of Raj and Pookie. Damn, Fess must be at it again! This time I didn't bother with my .22. Lana closed the dogs in her room. Half-awake but fully perturbed, we headed for the sunporch.

Even over the alarm signal, we heard Fess's churrs and squeals. Just what I needed at this hour—Cacophony in Dammit Minor. On autopilot, we grabbed coats and gloves for anti-raccoon body armor, then Lana hovered behind me as I opened the sunporch door.

A fetid, musky odor assaulted us. Fess had knocked his cage on its side and was thrashing about inside it. The door from the sunporch to our backyard was ajar. And an exquisite black-and-white banded snake vibrated its tail at us.

I wasn't as shocked to see a snake this time; in fact, I was beginning to feel like an extra on Animal Planet. "Call 911, then bring me the gun from my night stand," I directed Lana. "I'll turn off the alarm."

We met back at the sunporch a few minutes later where I kept a watchful eye on the snake.

"The gun?" I whispered, reaching out my hand.

"I didn't get it."

I took my eyes off the snake for a moment and raised an eyebrow at her.

"If I bring you your gun, you'll go wandering around the backyard, and who knows who's out there? The cops are on the way."

To give credit where Bank of America might not, a patrol car and an Animal Control truck pulled up quite promptly. Two uniforms searched the grounds while an older gent wearing an Animal Control jacket and carrying snake tongs walked into the sunporch.

"Oh, king snake," he pronounced right away. "Not poisonous. But they can bite." Within a few seconds he had the snake's head secured in the tongs.

As he lifted it from the floor, Lana pointed to the snake's belly where something red contrasted sharply with the creature's clean black-and-white markings. "Is that blood?"

The man turned the snake over. On its belly, bright red laundry marker spelled out a warning: STOP ASKING QUESTIONS . . . OR ELSE.

21

KARJALAPASTI

Darlene had invited me over for dinner, her way of thanking me for the "rescue." She made an honest to God pot roast—scrumptious! She passed along two medical journals from the hospital library with articles on new cancer research. Such culinary delight contrasted directly with my experience when I came home from work the day before my surgery. I walked into the house and my nostrils practically spasmed. Ugh, what was that smell? This, um, aroma, was wafting from the vicinity of the kitchen. I poked my head in there. "Hi. How's it going?"

Lana stirred a pot. "Good. I'm making you something special since you'll have hospital food for the next few days."

"What is it?" I lifted lids and snooped, but couldn't determine the contents. One pot looked like potatoes with orange and purple things and smelled fishy. The skillet held a number of mystery meats and smelled mostly like dill.

"It's a surprise," she answered.

Oh, great. Once when she surprised me, she served spelt flavored with squid ink. She'd heard it was an Italian delicacy, and figured because I'm part Italian, I'd like it. Her heart is always in the right place, but her palate navigates poorly. To get my mind off dinner I asked, "What did you do with your day?"

"Oh, I vacuumed the dogs, mopped the ceiling, and baptized the winter vegetable garden."

"Steam-cleaned your sense of humor, too, I see. Judging by your high spirits, I'd say you've also spent time with a certain soccer player." I knew the arrow hit home when she blushed. Of course at our age it could be an early hot flash.

"OK, I saw Nate, and –didn't you notice? I bought some Thanksgiving cards and did some Qi Gong. Mostly I relaxed. Saturn's at a critical conjunction this time of the year; it's important to de-stress. How was your day? How did the pre-op go?"

"Dr. Winter called me a problem patient. She wants me to cut back on coffee; says a study shows coffee stimulates estrogen and some breast cancers feed on estrogen. I tried to get out of the pre-op blood test. I told her if any of my lymph nodes are unaffected, I want to keep them, and—"

"I can't imagine why she called you a problem patient."

I ignored her jibe. "And when it comes to anesthesia, I want the gas mask first, *then* the IV; not visa versa. That way I won't be awake for the needle stuff."

"Who won the battles?"

"I agreed to cut back a little on coffee. I gave in on the pre-op blood test. I passed out; it was hideous." I lifted my sleeve and showed her the gauze pad inside my elbow where they'd done wildcat drilling. "She caved on sparing as many lymph nodes as possible. She said it was risky, but she finally agreed. And it's up to the anesthesiologist to decide whether to give me gas before the IV. I won't see him until just before surgery tomorrow."

Lana put two plates on the table and I went to wash up. I changed into a sweater, jeans, and my new black boots. I brushed my hair. I was looking good today, rather like a middle-aged Isabella Rossellini. Some days I favored her considerably, but on bad hair or bad attitude days, I looked more like Dwight Yoakam in drag. I gave myself a final glance in the mirror and marched to the culinary guillotine awaiting me.

Lana lit two candles and set places with our best silver. A Joan Armatrading CD played in the background, one of my favorites. She filled our plates with her concoction. "What would you like to drink? Tea? Ginger ale? Wine?"

I wanted to ask 'Why are you being so sweet? Could it be because I'm really, really sick and you feel sorry for me? Or is it because you love me, plain and single? I mean simple.' But when I tossed back my Rossellini locks what I said was, "Zinfandel's good." I waited until she put our drinks on the table and sat down. "I think somebody's stalking Darlene."

"Why on earth would you think that?" she asked.

"How did this Rattler Man know where Darlene was living? She just moved. Either he has access to police records or he's been watching her, following her. Stalking. One of the psych profiles of the killer was a stalker, remember? What if Darlene was the intended victim all along?"

She cocked her head. "How could that be?"

"Well, if the attacker is stalking Darlene, it means one of two things: either he had a hate vendetta against both women, or he killed Belle Farby by mistake. There's a fifty-fifty chance it's Darlene he's been after."

"I hadn't thought of that," she remarked. And before I could head it off at the pass: "How do you like the *karjalapasti*?"

I might not have the Finnish name exactly right, but it sounded something like that. Whatever it was, there was a heap of it on my plate. I had managed three mouthfuls and I didn't think I could manage much more. "I'm not very hungry tonight. Sorry. I had a late lunch."

Lana cleared my dish without breaking the plate over my head. There is a God. She poured us green tea and placed a dish in front of each of us with an anisette cookie, a sprig of mint, and peach slices artfully arranged.

As we finished dessert Lana said, "Tess, do you think maybe you're playing detective to avoid facing painful feelings?"

That hit the Stooge on the noggin. "What if I am? We all have our ways of coping. Isn't mine legitimate if it gets me through this and doesn't hurt anybody?"

Lana leaned across the table and took my hand. "You're having a mastectomy tomorrow morning, Tess. You need to let it out."

I wanted to let it out. But on some level I was still watching a movie of a woman named Tess who was going to lose her left breast tomorrow.

Which was perhaps better material than what we had available on the seventy-odd channels we clicked through after we cleaned up the kitchen and walked the dogs. The night's offerings left something to be desired: two old Clint Eastwood movies; the Shopping Channel; a politician explaining how he can be compassionate and still vote against banning the purchase of Uzis by twelve-year-olds; a pseudo-investigative show discussing all the references to UFO's in the Bible; a UCSD TV lecture on psoriasis; and an interview with a football player whose salary is greater than the GNP of Benin. And we wonder why our national IQ is declining.

We were trying to decide on the lesser of all programming evils when the phone rang. Lana answered it. "Yes, just a minute." She passed the phone to me.

"Who is it?" I mouthed. She shrugged an 'I don't know.' Telemarketers can be very clever, so I answered cautiously. "This is Tess."

"Tess Camillo?" a nervous, male voice asked.

"Yes; who's this?"

"I hear you're interested in Belle Farby's murder," he began.

If this was a telemarketer, he had a great angle. "Who is this?"

"Sorry; can't tell you that right away. We need to build trust first. I'm calling because I sense you genuinely care about this woman's murder."

"I care about punishing the murderer."

"Good. I work as a phone psychic. I know, you probably think we're all frauds. But the truth is I do have certain abilities." He hesitated, as though he were struggling with a decision. "I've been getting messages about Belle Farby's murder. Flashes, glimpses, clues. It's hard to explain, but I think I can help. I'm sure the police won't take me seriously, so I thought I'd try you."

His voice was a little light in the larynx. Was he a friend of Roark's? "I need to know who you are," I urged.

"Not now. I'm picking up something about your feet. Slippers? Shoes? No, wait—boots. With spurs or buckles, I don't know, something silver."

I looked down at my boots with their sparkling butch buckles and chains. A chill slid down my spine. I tuned back into the conversation.

"Anyway, back to why I called." He paused for breath, but not for long. "Tell the police this: I'm getting the image of a fingerprint in the middle of the woman's forehead. And a snake's rattle in her jeans pocket. If I'm wrong about this, I'll drop the whole matter. But if I'm right, maybe the cops'll want to hear what I have to say. I don't want any money or publicity; I just want to help. By the way, I sense you'll be gone for a while. Something to do with your health. I'll be sending you healing light. In a little while I'll call again. And save yourself the Star69 charge; I'm at a pay phone and I'm leaving." The receiver clicked.

I had the oddest feeling when he hung up. Like electric tingles all over my body. Like he was standing nearby, watching me. Woo woo stuff.

Woo woo or voodoo, it was just what the doctor ordered. Maybe not Dr. Winter or my plastic surgeon, but some Great Healer in the Sky knew precisely how to distract me from the anxiety of surgery the night before I would lose a breast.

I knew the print of Belle's own index finger had been found on her forehead and a snake's rattle was in her pocket. The police had withheld this information from the public; no way could the psychic have discovered these facts from a newspaper article or casual study of the murder. Yet somehow he knew.

I told Lana about my conversation with the psychic. She showed little surprise, as if psychics sensed these things every day. Next time she wants to find her missing turquoise skirt, nail polish, eggbeater, or address book, maybe I'll suggest she consult a psychic.

I phoned the SDPD. I knew Kari would be gone at this hour, but I left an intriguing voice mail message for her about the psychic's "insights." I also told her I was having cancer surgery tomorrow and she should contact Lana for further information. That would put starch in her bloomers.

The adrenaline rush of the psychic's call lasted more than an hour, but eventually emotional exhaustion and an excess of Eastwood caught up with me. I said good night to Lana and went to my bedroom. Raj must have sensed something; he became particularly attentive and affectionate. I petted his warm head and scratched behind his ears. I took his face in my hands. "Raj, old buddy, I'm going away for a few days." I noticed several gray hairs around his muzzle. Raj wasn't a young pup anymore. Neither was I. Mortality sucks.

I blasted the shower water, letting it beat steamy and hot all over my body. Almost instantly I began to cry—big wet sobs from somewhere awfully deep. What will my body be like? How will I live in it? What will it feel like? What will look back at me when I stand naked in front of the mirror? Will I be so scarred no one will ever want to touch me again?

In bed, I ran my hands over my left breast and felt the ominous lump. The last night I have two real breasts, I thought, and there's no lover to press them against. I'd considered inviting Lee Anne to stay the night, but our intimacy level was *Annie Hall* and this night required *The Hours*.

Lana opened my door. Without a word, she slipped in bed beside me and snuggled into my body. I couldn't call what happened making love but the next morning when I climbed onto the operating table and the gas mask came down, I felt at peace, karjalapasti or no karjalapasti.

22

ST. FRANCIS
OF ARACHNIA

I looked like Edward Scissorhands's ugly cousin. Five long plastic drain tubes extended from my chest and belly, each ending in a squeezable rubber bulb. My left breast had left the building along with Elvis and half of my lymph nodes. Surgeons had tunneled abdominal tissue through my trunk to replace the breast. As I'd been forewarned, some nerves had been severed and others traumatized. Even my belly button had shifted a few degrees latitude.

I signed myself out of the hospital two days early, against the doctors' wishes. Lulled by Percocet and by whatever anesthesia might still be in my system, I spent my time sitting or dozing on the living room sofa.

The lab was analyzing tissue from the excised lymph nodes to see how far the cancer had spread. Dr. Winter stopped removing nodes when they looked unaffected, but only the lab results would tell us what was really going on.

What I hadn't told anyone but knew from my doctors was that for any lobular invasive breast cancer tumor over five centimeters, the odds of the cancer spreading to the lymph nodes were so great that even with surgery, chemo, *and* radiation, chances of surviving more than five years were only about 30 percent. My tumor had measured nine centimeters.

My fourth day home I made, perhaps, a slight error in judgment. I wanted to wean myself from narcotic meds but still had considerable pain, especially with the abdominal incision. Lana is resourceful with all kinds of herbs. I figured if I developed a new take on 'medical marijuana' and downed plenty of ibuprofen, I could eliminate the narcotics.

That afternoon Lana was out at a community college class learning about Apaches and Zunis. I'd smoked a gorilla-sized joint and was out playing hopscotch on the rings of Saturn.

I heard a knock at the door. Through the peephole I spied three conservatively dressed black women. The older one in the middle looked like she hadn't laughed in ten years; the two younger ones looked resigned.

What I did next can only be understood in the emotional context of the moment. Not only was I high on marijuana; I was very high on life. Silky strands of support, prayers, casserole dishes, well wishes, cards, flowers, calls, concern, and hugs from friends, coworkers, and family suspended me in healing and joy. St. Francis of Arachnia, the most benevolent spider in the Land of Metaphors, had spun me a web.

So there I was with tubes emerging from my belly and a roach in the ashtray, feeling ebulliently gracious toward all humankind, including the three strangers on my doorstep.

OK, even stoned I knew they were Jehovah's Witnesses, but I couldn't quite remember why it might not be a good idea to invite them in.

I opened the door. The one on the right sniffed the air, fragrant with bouquet of weed. The one on the left clutched *Awake* and *Watchtower* magazines. The older one's eyes fixed on my blood-filled drain tubes. Blood, I recalled from a comparative religions course, has certain taboo associations for Witnesses. For perhaps the first time in history, three Jehovah's Witnesses were speechless.

Fighting the ganja giggles, I asked, "Can I help you?"

Gladys and her two Pips recovered. The older one said, "We're part of a free Bible study group in your neighborhood; we'd like to tell you about it. May we come in?"

I signaled Raj and Pookie to be cool, opened the door wide, and gestured toward the smoke-filled living room. "Come on in. Make yourselves comfortable. I'm recovering from breast cancer surgery and can't be on my feet much, so I'm going to crash right here." I sank into my favorite spot on the couch and looked at the women expectantly. They entered but didn't sit down.

Gladys gathered herself and said, "I'm so sorry to hear about your illness. Did you know that in God's original plan there would be no sickness in the world?"

"Wow. He must be really pissed that His plans weren't followed. Do you think He'll sue the contractors?" My mind just couldn't quite wrap around how you're supposed to converse with Jehovah's Witnesses.

The Pips didn't know whether to run or buy real estate. Gladys glanced at the menorah on the fireplace mantel, a family heirloom that's always displayed. "Exactly what religion do you follow, if you don't mind me asking?"

That's a difficult question even when I'm not stoned, and right then I didn't know what condition my condition was in. Judaism is determined by the mother; true—I swear on a stack of latkes. But my mother's relatives, the Kragers, Dutch jewelers who'd been in the U.S. for four generations, barely attended synagogue. While Kinky Friedman may be a Texas Jew-Boy, I'm not sure I'm a Jersey Jew-Girl.

On my Dad's side, the Camillos had been staunch Catholics until a priest allegedly copped a feel from my great-aunt when she was sixteen, at which point they converted en masse to the Baptist church. To prevent a marital rift, my parents had agreed that sons would be raised Jewish; daughters, whatever the Camillos deemed proper. My father turned my religious education over to Grandma Camillo, who saw to it that I scorched my butt in fundamentalist pews every Sunday morning.

Intellectually I'd long ago shed Biblical literalism, but on a far deeper level I remain a believer. I believe faith is more powerful than any laser, defibrillator, nano-quantum crystal, or media conglomerate. I believe the only meaningful way to save the world is to change hearts one at a time. I believe in God, the Tao, and the Zen of zip.

As I ran all this through my THC-laced lobes, I forgot exactly what it was Gladys had asked me. Something to do with religion—how many angels can dance on the head of a Magic Wand? Bear in mind, my mind wouldn't bring rational thought to bear. When I finally remembered the question, I pulled an answer out of the cosmos. "I'm an Etruscan."

Gladys didn't like that answer one little bit but she hadn't encountered a pot-smoking Etruscan who'd had a mastectomy before. No doubt she'd bring it up at the next meeting. "If you'd like to join our Bible study group, it meets on Thursdays at 7:00 P.M. We'll pray to Jehovah for your recovery." She handed me a card with a Kingdom Hall address printed on it.

She and the Pips stood there. I sat on the couch looking at the card. Neither one of us, oh, neither one of us, wanted to be the first to say good-bye. Finally, Gladys gestured meaningfully to one of the Pips, who left a copy of *Awake* magazine on the end table for me, and they headed for the door.

"Have a happy Thanksgiving!" I said out of habit, about two seconds before I remembered that Witnesses don't celebrate holidays. I had a reserved hot seat in Witness hell now for sure.

An hour later I'd pretty much come back down to earth. I distracted myself from incision pain with an episode of Days of Our Thighs. A commercial blared, "Remember, your holidays aren't complete without green bean casserole!" How did we go from grateful pilgrims and a messiah in a manger to mandatory vegetable dishes? Should've asked Gladys. Suddenly the phone rang again.

"Tess Camillo, please?"

I recognized Dr. Winter's voice: the lab results! My throat, tonsils, and trachea went into nickel back formation. "It's me, Dr. Winter. What's the news?"

"The margins of your tumor were completely clear. And in spite of their irritated, inflamed appearance, the lab found no sign of cancer cells in any of the lymph nodes I removed.

You had a nine-centimeter invasive carcinoma that somehow never spread."

"Thank God!"

"Nevertheless, with a tumor that size, I advise you to begin taking the medicine I told you about right away."

"The drug that'll throw me into instant menopause, dry me up like a prune, and might increase my risk of other cancers? I'll think on it," I replied. Dr. Winter was bemoaning my lack of cooperation when I finally absorbed what she'd just told me. "Are you *sure* about those lab results?"

"I didn't believe it at first so I had them run the lab tests twice. That's why it took so long. We didn't want to give you false hope. But now we're sure. Tess, you're our poster child for miracles."

One heartbeat will be your last. It takes faith to believe that any effort—clean living, seat belts, good nutrition, prayer—can influence which heartbeat that will be. Did the energy behind the love and prayers I received somehow zap the cancer cells? I don't have all the answers. I only know that Mystery blesses; that our awareness of mortality influences our hope, joy, relationships, and satisfaction. In other words, this is important. Don't trust it to the man who wears the star; most likely his CEO's being indicted. Trust it to the One who made the stars. Take it from a poster child.

With threat of death, life had become especially sweet. In her last breathing moments, as someone held the world's most venomous snake to her neck, I wondered: did Belle Farby sense that sweetness?

23

SKY FACE

The nex afternoon I was rummaging for an as-yet unread magazine and listening to NPR when the phone rang. "Hello?"

"Hey, girl, it's me. How ya holdin' up?" Kari spoke with a gentleness I'd only heard her use with her kids.

"Not too bad, considering my bod's more screwed up than a Halliburton audit. Thanks for the flowers. I guess you got my message?"

"Yeah, pretty damned interesting. Did this guy ask for money?"

"No. Said he didn't want publicity either."

"Well, that makes him different from most so-called psychics. A homicide sergeant's handling the Farby case now. I told him about your call. He's not against exploring this but he doesn't want the media to know. If one of us follows up, we'll have to file a report, and the media's good at sniffing out paper trails. So . . ." Kari paused to see if I was following, then continued, "I know you're not going to be up for anything right away, girl, but when you're ready the sergeant wants to know if you'd be willing to meet this guy. Size him up, get whatever information you can."

I had a semi-official investigative assignment. Righteous! "Anything specific you want me to ask him?"

"Yeah. 'Who murdered Belle Farby?'" She laughed. "These psychic types rarely answer direct questions. See if you can at least find out where she was murdered. If we could get evidence techs to a crime scene, we might find something. Mainly we need to know if this guy's just yanking our chain."

"Will do."

"One more thing, and this is important: If he's not legit, he knows too much. Be sure to tell me when and where you set the meeting. We'll put plainclothes officers in unmarked cars in the area. And watch your ass, OK?"

"OK." Fatigue was creeping up on me and I stifled a yawn. Kari heard it and took the hint, signing off quickly. Trang and Celeste were coming over for dinner. I decided to rest so I'd be alert for their visit.

About 4:00 P.M, I awoke to see Lana toting her massage table to the front door. She leaned the table in its pale blue carrying case against the sill and said, "I've got a massage client, so I'm heading out. I should be home before Trang and Celeste get here. Need anything before I go?"

"I'm fine, thanks." She exited, stage right. I heard the growl of her ancient truck's engine and its substantial roll down the block.

I catnapped a while. When I woke up I fought boredom by reviewing my notes on the murder. Paging through the information, I was reminded of how ritualistic, maybe even fetishistic, the crime scene appeared: twenty-two old buttons, 197 strands of hair, a body lying on palm fronds, and a snake rattle in the pocket. Something about those buttons teased my forebrain. But what? My ruminations ended with a doorbell ring. I looked through the front door security peephole and did something I almost never do: I let a strange man into the house.

It's hard to say exactly what made me open the door, but when I did, we assessed each other for a few seconds without speaking. He was about five feet, ten inches, early to mid-thirties, slender but strong. He wore a blue and maroon rugby shirt and navy Dockers. His lampblack eyes belonged in a Native American face, watching eagles fly. Though on the surface quite masculine, something about his careful grooming and buffed out body signaled he was gay. Raj and Pookie hovered near me, but neither barked. He offered his hand. "My name's Trevor Tribeca. I'm the psychic who called you about the Belle Farby murder."

So much for Kari's plainclothes cops in unmarked cars. "Tess Camillo. Come on in." He smelled like freshly sliced apples. I hobbled back to my nest on the couch. "I usually don't wear drains, but my tuxedo's at the cleaner's."

"I sensed you weren't in much shape to travel. I thought it would be easier if I made the effort." An easy smile rode sidesaddle across his face. And oh, what a face!

It reminded me of a time I drove through New Mexico heading west at sunset. The sky turned all the colors of ripe peaches. Suddenly in the distance I saw big, bold spikes of lightning. The storm was so far away I couldn't hear thunder or see rain. But those jagged bright bolts against the peach sunset created a sacred visual for me.

Trevor's face was like that New Mexican sky—open, natural, glowing. And he had a lightning bolt. An old scar—faint purple in some places—ran from the corner of his left eye down his cheek to his lower jaw. It was the kind of scar you couldn't *not* notice.

He settled himself into a comfortable chair. "Was I right about the fingerprint on her forehead and the rattle in her pocket?"

"Put it this way: The police are interested in what you have to say."

"Well, before we get to that, I brought you a little something—kind of a get-well gift." He held out a small box.

I didn't want to look a Trojan Horse in the mouth so I accepted the gift.

"Go on, open it," he urged.

The box was the right size for a tongue stud from a silver-tongued devil. I didn't think a snake could fit inside. I unwrapped it and removed a pair of kitschy earrings. Each earring was about an inch square, bright red, with yellow polka dots painted on it. Cute, but not me. I thanked him anyway.

Pookie rubbed against Trevor's leg. Even Raj moved a little closer. Pookie would suck up to Charles Manson, but I'd never seen Raj take to a stranger like this.

"Do you know much about the psychic hotline business, Tess?"

"Enough not to call one."

He laughed. "I don't think you're our typical customer. Most of our customers have, um," he searched for the right word, ". . . issues. The people who run hotlines are in business to make money. They train us to keep customers on the line as long as possible. But we do try to help them if we can." He paused to gather thoughts. "Sometimes I really *can* help. And not just the hotline customers, but others. The feeling comes on subtle . . . when I get into that . . . place; it's like the barometric pressure change in the air right before a rainstorm. Every cell is revved up and I get this sense of expectancy." He petted the dogs. "Guess I've always been kind of weird. I was the kid who got picked last for baseball games."

"I was good at softball. I should get back into that." I looked down at my body cocooned in gauze and bandages. "When I'm healed, I mean."

"And you will be healed. You're going to be well and strong. I *know* this."

I wanted to believe it with all my heart. I looked him in the eyes and decided if he was a con man, he was awfully good. "I hope you're right," I said and wondered for the eighteenth time how he got that scar.

"Anyway, this state of mind . . . it's been giving me information about this woman's murder."

"Well, don't keep me in suspense: Who killed Belle Farby?" I half-joked.

"I wish I could tell you," he said simply.

"From reading the papers you probably know Belle's body was moved to UCSD after she was murdered. Do you have any idea where the actual murder took place?"

"No, not yet. But if the police suspect some particular location, I'm willing to go there and see if I pick up anything," he offered.

"I'll talk to the cops about that. What *can* you tell us about the murderer?"

"It was definitely a man. And he lives or works somewhere near ocotillo cactus. Every time I receive these, uh, messages about the murderer, ocotillos are part of the vision."

Borrego Desert, home of Mongoose Matthews, is full of ocotillos.

24

FRANKIE
AND THE GANG

A deviant version of Crocodile Dundee opened the front door and smiled. I held up the Bureau of Indian Affairs ID card I'd mocked up with a color printer and the office laminator. "Hi, I'm Tess Camillo from the Bureau of Indian Affairs. I'm here for our meeting."

He eyed me slowly; no sign of recognition. "What meeting?"

"You didn't get our letter?" He just stood there, eyes taking me in. I continued, "Your home is situated on the burial ground of one of the Vejaskume tribal chiefs. The site dates to about 1789. We want this land for a dig. I've been sent to negotiate fair compensation for your property."

Wade "Mongoose" Matthews stood a nimble, lean five feet, nine inches with wild blond hair and a matching mustache. His blue eyes had a hint of *Deliverance* in them. With his outdoor tan, denim, boots, and engaging grin, this known rapist was just the kind of guy women could fall for, based only on hormones, pheromones, and potential provocation of other moans.

I had every reason to think he might be dangerous to women in other ways, too. When I'd pulled up to his property, I'd immediately noticed a front yard of indigo bush, barrel cactus, and five towering ocotillos. Matthews was by far the most likely suspect in Belle's murder, if only I could break his dentist appointment alibi. And figure out how he was connected to Belle Farby or Darlene Nealson.

He looked me up and down several times but never checked the ID card. Finally he said, "Come on back to my workshop and we'll talk."

Two minutes later, he was the one doing the talking.

"There was this pioneer family—you know, like Daniel Boone and Davy Crockett—and they were living in a cabin," he said as he grasped a rattlesnake right where the snake's neck would be if it had one. "And one day, the man of this family brings in wood from the woodpile and drops dead in his tracks. No one knows why. The oldest son and the mother take him out and bury him. According to tradition the son inherits his father's pocket watch, boots, straight edge razor, and his one good suit. Life goes on."

Mongoose Matthews picked up a small tool that resembled a crochet hook. He lifted the snake's upper jaw with the instrument, revealing its fangs, then positioned the snake next to a glass funnel that drained into a Mason jar. The jar was packed in ice. With practiced casualness, he snapped the snake's fangs over the edge of the funnel and massaged its venom glands. "About a month later, the son who inherited is out in the field plowing and he suddenly keels over dead. Like father, like son."

Matthews adjusted the position of his thumb and index finger on the venom glands. Butter yellow venom streaked one side of the funnel. I have to start hanging out with a better class of people.

"C'mon, Frankie, I know you can do better'n that," he muttered.

"This snake's name is Frankie?"

"All my snakes are named Frankie," he replied with what I had to admit was a charming smile. His fingers pressed more insistently on the snake as he continued his story. "The next oldest boy helps his mother bury the older brother, and he inherits the manly possessions of the family. This time the kid only lasts a week or so, then he goes out like a light."

How could he shoot the breeze while milking a rattler? It was like reggae dancing in the middle of a Pap smear.

"By now, the mother starts putting things together. She tells her only remaining son to get a knife and split open the soles of her dead husband's boots. There, snagged inside the leather, were rattler fangs that still contained traces of venom. When the wearer of the boots stepped the wrong way, the fangs pushed through the sole and they got bit. The moral of the story?" He paused for effect. "It's easy to die with your boots on!" He stomped his own cowboy boots and laughed so hard I was afraid he'd drop the snake.

"Could that really happen?" I asked.

"Hell, no. Rattler venom isn't so potent that a few traces would drop you on the spot. But it's a good story."

"Who buys all this venom?" I inquired.

"Mostly the drug companies that make antivenin. And research outfits."

"Someone's researching rattlesnake venom?"

"Oh, you'd be surprised." Matthews dropped Frankie into a plastic trashcan, where, from the smell of things, an American Bandstand of Frankies danced the Philadelphia Funk. With a special pole, he lifted another Frankie from a nearby cage and positioned the snake for milking. "They use snake venom in pain research, disease research, um, cancer research. Few years back, one British company couldn't buy enough of it from me. Said the shape of a molecule of something in rattler venom was the same as the molecule of cancer cells." He fit the snake's fangs over the edge of the funnel. "My friend Jack in Tampa, they're buying copperhead venom off him for breast cancer research."

Snake venom and breast cancer research in the same sentence? OK, Universe, you got my attention.

When Frankie II was drained to the last drop, Matthews slipped the snake into the trashcan, washed his hands in the garage sink, dried them with a paper towel, and lit a Lucky Strike. "What was the one thing the Vejaskume always buried inside the graves with their dead?"

I'd done everything I could to look the part of an overworked female bureaucrat just trying to do her job. I had on a charcoal pants suit, a pink silk blouse, pearl earrings, and makeup. I'd dyed the gray out of my hair and had a good cut. I'd fixed myself up for the first time since my surgery and I looked damned good, all things considered.

What I didn't do was bone up for a quiz. I'd skimmed Lana's notes from her class on Southwest Native American cultures, but damned if I could remember what the Ve-jaskume buried with their dead. An animal totem? A basket? Clean underwear? When in doubt, fake it. "Food. For the next life. Every corpse was buried with at least a small food supply," I stated matter-of-factly.

"The Vejaskume never buried food with their dead," he stated just as matter-of-factly. He sent a few smoke rings toward heaven; God would need some Glade. "What are you're really here for?"

My drains were out but the pain was still in. It strained my ab incision to stand tall but I pulled my five feet, five inch posture to about six foot one. I looked him in the eyes and tried to lie as convincingly as the Warren Commission. "I've already explained. Do you want to see the letter asserting the BIA's right of eminent domain? It's out in my car."

I could tell from his eyes he wasn't buying any of it. Uh oh.

Without a word, he led the way from his workshop-garage back into his house. Matthews settled into the over-stuffed maroon leather seat of an antique barber chair that dominated his living room.

"Oh, come on, I was just testing you," I said. "I wanted to see if you were familiar with the indigenous cultures native to the Borrego area. Seems you are, so you'll understand the necessity for the BIA to acquire this property."

He brought an ashtray up from the floor, balanced it on muscular denim-clad thighs, and tapped some ashes into it. This time he blew his smoke my way. "Oh, I'm familiar with the local tribes, all right. The question is, if you're from the BIA, why aren't you? The Vejaskume *do* bury food with their dead."

Well, s-h-t and three-quarters. "OK, you got me." I grinned and lowered my eyes. "I'm new to the area. I moved here a few weeks ago. I'm divorced." I swallowed hard and tried to look embarrassed; after all, he was at least ten years my junior. "I heard from some friends that there was this hunky guy who had converted the old Dairy Queen building into a house. When you get to be my age, you can't afford to pass up opportunities. I'm not a bar person, and I couldn't think of a way to meet you, so . . ." I let my voice trail off and batted my eyes at him.

Thank God for the male ego. He almost visibly began to think with his penis. "Want a beer?"

"Sure." I smiled at him.

He returned from the kitchen with a can of Coors for each of us; no glasses. He walked up to me. I don't know what I'd expected, but it wasn't the kiss on the mouth he delivered. "I know how to pump other things besides venom, babe. I got condoms if you feel like a little recreation."

I turned away to keep from laughing in his face. If this guy got one look at the incisions and bandages under my clothes, he'd shit himself and I knew it. I stood up, took a taste of Coors, longed for Corona, and gazed out his front window at the ocotillos. Matthews had had so many encounters with the law that I hadn't had time to absorb all the background in his files. "You sure know a lot about the Vejaskume. Were you raised here in Borrego?"

He'd settled back in the barber chair. "Been here thirteen years in March. I grew up in Florida. Got sick of bugs, so I moved out here."

Bugs bothered him? This from a man who was more intimate with rattlesnakes than I was with my own brother?

"Thirteen years is a long time. You must have friends in Julian, too."

"Plenty. Why?"

"I need a dentist, a dry cleaner, a hairdresser. I'll probably have to go in to Julian for some things. I figured if you have friends there, I could give them my business."

"I got some friggin' tight friends in Julian. Let's go dancing there Saturday night; I'll introduce you around."

"Actually, I'm booked this weekend. Next week maybe."

"Suit yourself."

"I do need to see a dentist soon. My back molar is killing me."

"Try Tom Eakins in Julian. Good guy, and he's got one of those quiet laser drills." He drained half a can of beer in one swallow. "'Scuse me a sec. I gotta get that venom into dry ice or it won't be worth a damn." He returned to the workshop.

I used his absence as an opportunity to Sherlock. The living room and eat-in kitchen—the only rooms I could access without arousing suspicion—were, like the man himself, fascinatingly off kilter.

He'd preserved the old Dairy Queen fountain area in his living room with its metal bins for nuts and sprinkles, and pumps for syrup. The bins were now planters and the pumps held plant food and water. One bin contained a healthy Wandering Jew. His neo-Nazi sensibilities apparently weren't attuned to horticulture. On one wood-paneled wall hung a knife collection, full of glittering dirks and exquisite daggers. He hadn't invested in a sofa, only a wooden rocker, ottoman, TV, the barber chair, and a bookshelf.

A bleached animal skull, probably coyote or fox, sunned itself on the window ledge above the kitchen sink. No radical posters espousing white supremacist ideals; no dirty pots, pans, or dishes. On the chipped oak dining table I found bills from Providian Visa and Magna Septic Tank Cleaners, a statement from Pacific Trust and Savings, a personal letter with a San Diego P.O. box return address, and junk mail. I heard a squeak of the floorboards. I slipped the personal letter into my pocket and turned around.

Matthews held a silver dagger to my throat.

25

FIGURE THE ODDS

"Gimme that," Matthews demanded.

His eyes and voice told me he'd use the knife, no question. I'd been cut up enough lately. I reached into my pocket slowly, retrieved the letter, and handed it to him.

He glanced at the letter, tossed it back on the pile of mail, and hissed, "What are you really about, bitch?"

"Sorry. I know it was stupid, but I saw it was personal and I wanted to know if it was from a girlfriend." I did my best to sound like a whiny woman who hadn't had sex since last Fourth of July.

He lowered the knife and slapped me hard across the face. "Get the fuck outta here!"

I saw him laughing to himself in my rear view mirror as I pulled away.

My cheek stung. Would it leave a mark? I didn't want Lana to know about this. I touched the place where he'd smacked me and felt the heat of my skin and something wet. Tears. Damn.

I hadn't snared much information, but as I cruised through the desert town of Borrego Springs toward State Road 3, I was glad I'd made the trip. Being cooped up after surgery these past few weeks made me lust for the outdoors. The air was so clean I wanted to suck up a lifetime supply. Except for the wind's low murmur, the entire area was quiet. Not big city quiet—truly still.

Boulders sequined the distant purple mountains. Creosote and mesquite scented the breeze while palms marked oases. After the winter rains, this arid expanse would bloom with yellow, purple, pink, and orange wildflowers. And scarlet ocotillo.

A raggedy coyote darted across the road ahead of me; I swerved just in time. He didn't seem flustered by the peril of four Pirellis. State Road 3 emptied onto Route 78 where mesas and arroyos in ochre, buff, and sage green gave way to sienna foothills, then to mountains covered with pine and black oak. I navigated twisty cutbacks until twenty-five minutes later when I entered the mountain tourist haven of Julian.

On Main Street, I passed a grocery with benches out front and an American flag snapping in the breeze. I continued past a bakery and an apple pie shop. Red shutters decorated the hearth store where residents shopped for wood stoves and fireplace pokers, and visitors browsed a plethora of trinkets. Horse-drawn buggies pulled tourists along the main avenue.

On the other side of Main Street between the Chuck Wagon Deli and a real estate office, I found what I was after—down a side street hung the shingle of Tom Eakins, D.D.S.

I parked nearby and climbed one flight of stairs to the office. A receptionist who'd been on the job about sixty-two years too many looked up from her computer screen. "Yes?"

"I was visiting my friend Wade Matthews in Borrego and this tooth—" I stuck my finger in my mouth, indicating a right molar, "—started hurting like crazy. I don't have an appointment, but Wade said Dr. Eakins might squeeze me into his schedule if he knew I was a friend of his."

Out of breath, I simulated a toothache grimace and waited for her answer. She buzzed someone on an internal phone line, mumbled into the receiver, then hung up. "Dr. Eakins can see you in about twenty minutes." The other two people patiently waiting in Eakins' office didn't seem overly thrilled with this news flash. The receptionist handed me a clipboard of forms and said, "You'll need to fill these out while you're waiting."

Like a first-year drama student, I slapped my hand to my forehead. "I left my insurance card in the car. I'll be right back."

I scooted the Silver Bullet out of town and onto the highway. On the way back to San Diego, as I cruised the peaceful rolling ranch land between Julian and Ramona, my mind played with probabilities. As a math major, I learned in Statistical Probability class that odds are never quite what they seem. In a room of twenty-three people, what's the probability two or more will have the same birthday? There are 365 days in a year, right? And thirty days in a month? Yet the odds are better than 50 percent.

What was the probability Matthews would know about the Vejaskume tribe's burial rites? What were the odds that a psychic would envision ocotillo cactus, so prominent in Matthews' front yard? Was it a statistically significant coincidence Matthews was buddies with the dentist who provided him an alibi for the day of Belle's murder? What was the probability I'd find out who killed her?

In all of my math courses I never learned formulas to calculate such things. But I was good at beating the odds.

26

WARM FUZZIES

Even in mild San Diego winters, Lana chills easily. As a kid she loved the warmth of those one-piece drop-seat Dr. Denton's. For her birthday gift last year, I Web surfed for a grown-up equivalent. Criminitlies, did I get a surprise! I had no idea what imaginative consenting adults could accomplish with drop-seat pajamas, but I was anxious to experiment. I ordered Lana a pair of size 10s in a blue sky/white cloud print.

She was wearing these new warm fuzzies when I returned home from Borrego that evening. I found her at the kitchen table, picking at rotisserie chicken, chips, and salsa. She looked up. "Why do people count sheep to fall asleep? I mean, why is counting sheep more boring than, say, counting gophers or counting fish?"

"Or Counting Crows?" I joked, alluding to a music group she liked. I grabbed a tortilla chip and plunged it into the salsa.

"Oh, by the way," I teased, "I kissed a very heterosexual man today." I savored her startled reaction. "This bra is rubbing against my incision. I need to go change." I started toward my room.

Like a train coming through a tunnel in the middle of the night, Lana's voice followed me down the hall. "Tess Camillo, you can't just tell me something like that then walk away!"

Laughing, I continued to my room. When I had removed the offending undergarment and donned a comfy sweat suit, I re-joined her for a cup of tea.

She poured boiling water from the kettle. "So who's this guy you kissed?"

"Actually," I told her, "I didn't kiss him; he kissed me." She put the kettle down. I had her full attention. "I spent almost an hour with Mongoose Matthews today, and that included a five-second kiss."

"Why would you let him do that?"

"He caught me by surprise," I said. Lana just looked at me. "Because I wanted information."

We finished a second cup of tea while I told her what I'd learned from Matthews. I strategically omitted the part about the knife he held to my throat.

Lana asked, "Were there ocotillos near his house?"

"Yup, big ones right in his front yard. 'Course, that's not exactly unusual out in Borrego. And I'm almost sure he didn't recognize me."

"Did you think he would?"

"If he put the king snake in the house, yes. Whoever did that knew I was asking questions about Belle's case. Which means he probably saw me either talking to Darlene or at the police station. Then he followed me so he knew where we

lived. Whichever way it happened, it stands to reason whoever put the king snake in our home would know what I look
like."

"Maybe." She tugged at the drop-seat in her pj's. "Have
you told Celeste anything about the psychic?"

"Called her about it last week. She didn't recognize
Trevor's name, but she said the psychic hotline he works for
actually is the most reputable one in the business. Of course,
that's like saying the octopus is the most intelligent mollusk."
I finished the chicken I'd put on my plate. "Said she picked
up a strange energy around Trevor."

Speaking of strange energy, Pookie was chasing either
dust motes or figments of her limited imagination. She kept
pawing the wall near my ankles and whining. She pulled back
a few paces, got a running start, and rammed her head smack
into the wall.

Lana cuddled the dazed dachshund. "Did Celeste give
you any specifics?"

"I'm not sure. You know how I get when she starts talking about 'bioplasmic streamers' and 'holarchies of universal
knowledge'." I let the thought trail while I finished rinsing
my cup. "I gotta call Kari about Trevor."

"Ocotillos . . . snakes . . . psychics . . . Sure is some weird
karma going on." Lana slid Pookie back on the floor.

"Weird karma, indeed." I dried my dishes while Lana got
the dogs fresh water. "Why did the killer sprinkle hair and
buttons on Belle's body? It's the kind of freaky thing a serial
killer would do. But if this Rattler Man is a serial killer, why
did he just warn us off with a harmless king snake?"

We stared while Raj and Pookie slurped from their

bowls, as if their wet noses and pink tongues could solve our riddles.

I continued. "Rattler Man's behavior certainly makes it seem more like the murder was personal, that he knew Belle. Or Darlene; whoever the intended victim was. And Arlo George—why did he bother with an alibi service? It's not like he's some classy CEO who's worried about his reputation. And—"

"Oh! That reminds me," Lana interjected. "You had a phone call. A Mrs. Virginia George wants you to call her back."

I knew from info Roark had forwarded that the cops had tracked Arlo George's actual whereabouts the day Belle was murdered. He'd been in the company of one Ruby Deelicious, a Bay Area stripper—one of those any-port-in-a-storm kind of women. The police had not divulged the Ruby Deelicious story to Mrs. George. I wondered why she wanted to talk to me. How did she know my name? How did she get my number? And what could she want, besides a different husband? I was about to find out.

27

VO5 INTIMACY

By the time I connected with Virginia George the next day, I'd learned three truths of life: Cottage cheese really *can* go bad if you keep it past its expiration date; it only takes a few weeks after major surgery for me to recover my libido; and sometimes the wrong spouse buys the alibi service.

From Catalina Boulevard, a right turn onto Lomaland Drive brought me thudding over the speed bump at the Visitor's Gate of Point Loma Nazarene College, where Virginia George had requested a two o'clock rendezvous.

The campus looks like Opie Goes to State filmed in paradise. I found a parking space overlooking a canyon that sloped down to the beach. Beyond that, a sapphire Pacific spattered with white sails stretched across the horizon. Overhead, crows rigorously protested the abundance of well-scrubbed students in their ecosystem. Ice plant and agapanthus separated sidewalk from canyon, and encircled a picnic table with a bench, a large wooden cross, and a sundial donated by the class of '45. The picnic table looked like a good place to wait.

Virginia George said to look for her in front of the admin building, a late Victorian structure across the street from where I sat. Its paint hinted of Stephen Foster songs, but its spiral staircase, Greek columns, and dome clearly preferred classical.

I'd been waiting twenty minutes when a vintage red Jaguar pulled up. Out stepped Virginia George: camel-colored wool slacks, white blouse, tartan vest, and hair on intimate terms with VO5 hairspray. She seemed agitated.

"Sorry I'm late," she offered as she joined me at the picnic table. "I'm probably just being paranoid, but . . . Well, you know some pieces of this and I know some pieces. I thought we might . . . Are you with the police?"

I laughed. "No, I'm a commercial database programmer." At her glazed look, I simplified. "I work with computers."

"Why are you involved with Belle's murder?" she asked bluntly.

"Long story. For starters, the detective in charge of the case is a friend of mine. I'm trying to help." Virginia George chewed on that for a moment and seemed satisfied. I sensed an opportunity. "You didn't say 'Ms. Farby's murder' or 'the lesbian's murder' or 'that woman's murder.' You said 'Belle's murder.' You knew her, didn't you?"

"When you asked me that day if I knew Belle Farby and I denied it, you knew I was lying. And I knew you knew." She stood up. "Let's walk." We headed toward the upper level of the campus.

Two crows overhead squawked loudly enough to be disruptive. I waited until their dispute was settled. "How do you know who I am?"

"Dear, I saw right through that little charade when you came to my house. I took down your license plate number." A strong breeze threatened her VO5 helmet. "I asked my nephew, who's good with Internet research, to find your phone number."

"So how did you know Belle?" Persistence, if not redundancy, was my friend.

"We shopped at the same grocery store. We always seemed to pick the same day to need an onion or run out of tartar sauce."

"Were you close?" I asked as we reached the crest of a hill.

Virginia George drew herself up to her full height, stopped, and turned toward me. She looked me in the eyes. "I didn't kill her." Passing students nodded greetings. One of their cell phones rang. Progress slowed while a girl told her mother she'd pick up Chinese on the way home. Virginia George fidgeted with her wedding ring as we waited for privacy.

When the students were gone, she took up where she left off. "When I was eighteen, my family took a vacation to Cape Hatteras. That's where I met Arlo. Oh, he was dashing—in full uniform, tan, handsome! I was dazzled by him; he was dazzled by my family's money." She hurried through the next sentences as if each word was a hot coal she must walk on. "I got pregnant. He did the expected thing and married me. Started drinking right after our daughter was born."

A crow dropped something shiny a few feet from us. I picked it up. An old Snapple bottle cap. Much as I might wish it, valuable clues apparently don't just drop out of the sky. Duh.

We wandered our way back to the picnic table. Virginia sat down on the bench across from me. "Why don't you just divorce your husband?" I asked.

"In my generation when we said 'till death do us part,' we meant it," she replied pointedly. "The only grounds for divorce in my church is adultery."

Amazing, the ties that bind. "So if Arlo cheated on you, you could divorce him?" I asked, mindful of Ruby Deelicious.

"I'd divorce him the minute I found out. He knows that, of course, and he'd lose every penny if it happened. My attorneys know how to circumvent community property laws."

That explained the alibi service. "So how does all this relate to Belle?"

A chunk of Virginia's personal tribute to lacquered aerosol whipped freely in the wind. I tried not to stare at it as she continued. "One day Belle and I were in line at the grocery deli and we struck up a conversation. She had a way about her, an independence . . ." Something changed in Virginia's voice. She patted her hair nervously. "I became curious—what did she know about life or relationships that I didn't know?"

We could probably fill the Marianas Trench with answers to that one, but I refrained from expressing this. I raised an eyebrow at Virginia. "You were attracted?"

"We never *did* anything!" she declared. "Belle and I went for tea a couple of times; we talked about our lives. I wanted to know more."

"And what did you find out?" I'll admit I was a bit titillated by the conversation. My post-surgical hormones were humming again.

"That I don't understand homosexuality. My church considers it a sin and I suppose it is. But she made me wonder."

I thought of how Belle probably reacted to a straight VO5 queen picking her up in the produce section and probing private matters. I smiled. "Did Arlo know Belle, too?"

She glanced over her shoulder to where her Jaguar was parked. There was no one around. "I'd mentioned her to him a few times. You know, 'I've met this new friend.' Not sure if he paid attention. But if Arlo and Belle did cross paths—after all, we only lived a few blocks apart—and if Arlo somehow felt threatened by her . . . Well, not when he's sober, of course, but, it's only two hours by air from San Francisco where the IMO conference was, to San Diego . . ." Her breathing was uneven; she was as frazzled as her hair looked. "I've been wondering if my husband is capable of murder."

28

DOMESTIC AFFAIRS

Way too many if's had to fall into planetary alignment for me to suspect Arlo seriously. Besides, I knew Ruby Deelicious provided a real alibi for our good old boy. I told Virginia George that I doubted her husband was a killer and resisted the temptation to disclose he was an adulterer. I slipped the Snapple lid into my pocket and headed home.

Along the way a water main had broken. The ensuing traffic jams provided time for mental doodling. Was Virginia George deliberately trying to shift suspicion onto Arlo? It was hard to get a read on her. At times she seemed self-contained, savvy, and cynical; at other times, frightfully naïve. Maybe she honestly believed she might be married to a murderer. If so, might murder join adultery as grounds for divorce? My mental doodles continued to squiggle around matrimony. To me, staying in a loveless marriage with a drinking alcoholic made about as much sense as Michael Jackson's nose, but to a naïve woman from an honorable Midwestern family who got pregnant out of wedlock in the Cleaver years, it apparently made perfect sense.

What made two individuals commit to the formidable yet indispensable concept of journeying through life together? Fear of loneliness? Emotional need? Family and societal pressure?

For the fourth time since I'd been at this intersection, the light turned green. I managed to advance another ten inches before it turned red again. I rolled down my window. The breeze had died down. I heard water from the broken main gushing onto the asphalt. A small plane buzzed overhead.

Suddenly I recalled a particular Spring afternoon when I was in fourth grade. My father picked me up from school and told me the two of us were going on a special adventure. This startled me because everyone in the family knew Dad wasn't particularly into parenthood. He viewed children much as he viewed kidney stones; you didn't want them but sometimes you got them anyway, they could be a real pain, and you looked forward to the day when they moved from your vicinity. If it hadn't been for Ma, the Baron and I would still be waiting for a stork to drop us in a fertile cabbage patch.

But every once in a while, something about being a parent clicked with Dad. This day his eyes were like Fourth of July sparklers. He drove us through Atlantic City and parked at the small airport called Bader Field.

Trained as a pilot in World War II, Dad towed TAN, DON'T BURN; USE COPPERTONE banners over Jersey beaches in bi-wing planes all summer, and flew fire bombing and mosquito spraying missions off-season. The rest of us had never flown. Our family vacations were road trips, and Dad's banner planes were off limits for all but professional purposes.

That day everything changed. Dad had bought his own

plane and he was taking me for a ride! This is about as good as it gets when you're nine years old.

Dad opened the door of his Stinson and I climbed in. The plane's cabin was cramped and smelled of leather seats and oily metal. Lights, buttons, gears, knobs, compasses, and altimeters mesmerized me. Dad started the engine, made sure my seat belt was buckled, and up, up we soared!

He steered us over my hometown, circling the island's lighthouse. He tipped one wing at City Hall, and pointed out the ant-like figures on my school's basketball court. I felt as though a noisy, congenial pterodactyl was taking me for a joy ride. I smiled so big and so often that my face muscles hurt.

On the drive home I burbled, "It's cool that you love flying, Dad! Is that why Ma married you?"

He patted me on the shoulder. "It's part of what she loves about me and part of what she hates about me." He lit one of the unfiltered Camels that eventually killed him, and blew smoke out the window.

That evening Ma made early dinner and shooed the Baron and me off to bed. Then she tore Dad a new asshole. He had taken every cent from their joint savings account and spent it on the plane. Without consulting her. Never mind the house needed a new roof. Never mind the car needed transmission work. Never mind college money for the kids. Her laments continued until her voice grew scratchy. Then she just sobbed.

I crept out of my bedroom, down the hall, and peeked at the two of them in the dining room. When Ma ran out of steam, Dad took her hand. "I live for three things," he said. "Mickey Mantle at bat, your kisses, and flying. I needed the plane, Eileen. Like I need you."

She laid her head on his shoulder and wept. This was my

first clue th at something about the intimacy of marriage could touch—and disturb—your deepest core.

By the time I got home, I was weary of both traffic and philosophizing. I poured my Tinker Toys out of their shiny container (an aluminum tube some administrations might see as proof of intent to build WMD); built two whatnots, one wouldabeen, and three thrillseekums, and rolled around on the floor with Raj and Pookie.

Thrashing on the floor with two dogs is not particularly conducive to healing incisions. Lana opened the living room door just as a sharp pain stabbed me. She caught the cringe.

"Aren't you supposed to be taking it easy?" She sat down on the sofa and looked at me, disapproval masking concern.

"How was your day?" I diverted the conversation as I put my Tinker Toys away.

"Pretty decent. One of my massage clients cancelled, though, so I had a few hours I didn't plan on. I went to the library. Want to see what I found?"

I've been around Lana long enough to know my cues. "Sure," I said, and sincerely hoped it wasn't an original Finnish recipe she planned to try tonight.

She dug into her shoulder bag, retrieved a piece of notebook paper, and handed it to me. "I thought maybe . . . well, since you decided not to do chemo or radiation, you might want to . . ."

She has lovely handwriting, like calligraphy. I skimmed her notes. They described alternative cancer therapies.

We settled in for a dinner of herbed turkey filets and green beans. No karjalapasti tonight, thank Zeus. While we ate, I read the information she'd given me. One possibility intrigued—Chinese herbs to boost the immune system so it could fight any remaining cancer cells on its own. Lana knew of a Chinese acupuncturist and gave me his card.

TV news was too depressing so I picked up the phone and called Kari. "Hey, you know that staunch alibi Mongoose Matthews gave you for the day Belle Farby was killed?"

"The dentist? We checked it out. Dentist vouched for him."

I shared with Kari my insight into how chummy the chomper specialist was with Matthews. "Crawl up his butt a bit. The alibi's probably bogus."

"I don't think it'll go anywhere, girl, but I'll see what I can do. Meanwhile, what did your psychic pal have to say about the crime scene?" she inquired.

"No dazzling insights, sorry. He did offer to check out Belle's house to see if it triggered anything."

"We might do that." She hesitated and I could almost see her squirming to find a way to introduce the next concept. "Um, my lieutenant talked to some folks up at the Berkeley Psychic Institute. There's a psychic ability test they want him to give this Trevor character. If he passes it, we'll use him on this case."

"I think he'll be OK with that. When I hear from him, I'll let him know."

The possibility of using Trevor's sensibilities to track a killer must have sparked a burst of adrenaline. I dashed off an e-mail to a breast cancer info portal asking about snake venom research, and took the dogs for a concrete constitutional. When I returned, I retreated to my room, stood up straight, and tried a few jumping jacks. My left arm wouldn't lift all the way; the area where some lymph nodes had been removed was too tender. But I did my best. And there in my humble bedroom I achieved a unique Zen state—I heard the sound of one boob bouncing.

29

BANE OF WALL STREET

Kari clunked a Diet Coke on the table between us and pushed the wet can in my direction.

I popped it open, drew a long sip, imagined (with little success) that the carbonation effervesced from Dom Perignon, and looked at her with anticipation.

Through a one-way window, Kari scrutinized Trevor Tribeca, who sat alone in the adjoining room, elbows propped on a desk. He had what Grandma Camillo called a case of the heebie jeebies, not unreasonable for a man whose psychic gifts were about to be tested by the skeptical San Diego Police Department.

A uniform entered the test room. He introduced himself to Trevor courteously, but his expression betrayed obvious homophobia. This crap of having to test some fairy who did Jeanne Dixon impersonations was only slightly less appealing than the way last Sunday's game had gone. Trevor covered his scarred cheek in his hand.

The cop opened a thick, oversized manila envelope he'd brought with him. Sixteen smaller sealed white envelopes slid out onto the desk in front of Trevor. Trevor picked one up and glanced at something written on it.

"What's on the envelopes?" I asked Kari.

"Numbers. One through sixteen."

"How's this work?" I inquired while two cockroaches engaged in a domestic dispute in the corner of the room, inches from my pants leg.

"Inside each envelope is either a police report of a violent crime, including a photo of the crime scene, and some trinket belonging to the victim, like a hair barrette. Or," Kari continued, "the envelope contains pages from the force newsletter, snapshots from a staff Halloween party, and a charm from one of my old charm bracelets." Kari noted my expression. "Nice touch, huh? Trevor is supposed to sort the sealed envelopes and sense which contain info on crimes."

The math major in me kicked in. "He has a 50-50 chance of getting each envelope right. He'd have to correctly identify at least nine of the sixteen to demonstrate ability versus luck."

"The Psychic Institute told us not to get excited unless he gets ten right."

Further discussion was distracted by Trevor. After handling one of the envelopes, he pushed his chair back from the table and looked like he was about to toss his cookies.

"You guys must have a pretty gross force newsletter," I cracked.

Kari looked somber. "What's the number on that envelope?" She didn't have the right angle to see.

"Umm . . . Thirteen."

She quickly scanned a reference sheet. "Thirteen is the Sally Debonnes case."

Sally Debonnes, a darling five-year-old, was raped, viciously mutilated, and strangled a few years ago. I looked away. The cockroaches were now carrying debris through a crack in the wainscoting, possibly crumbs from SDPD donuts.

Eventually Trevor indicated he was ready to leave. The sergeant asked if he wanted to wait for the test score. Trevor gave him a weak smile and said he was exhausted. As he turned to depart, I caught another glimpse of that horrific facial scar. My plastic surgeon, who built a breast out of belly jelly, could make Trevor look like he'd only nicked himself shaving. Maybe.

Trevor had one stylish loafer out the door when he stopped himself. Turning to the sergeant, he said, "There's a woman nearby. She has wounds, scars." He checked the sergeant's face for confirmation of his statement. The cop offered no feedback. Trevor continued, "She has to stop playing so rough with her dog or she'll open her stitches."

Caterpillars crawled up my spine; even Kari looked stunned. We entered the test room where the officer was scoring the test. "Don't blur the fingerprints," Kari admonished him.

He mumbled something that sounded like "Bite me."

"What's this about fingerprints?" I inquired. "I thought this was just a test of his psychic abilities."

"Trevor Tribeca is his professional name. This guy has used multiple aliases and he's moved around a lot. We haven't been able to confirm his real identity. I want to know who I'm dealing with."

"You're allowed to take his fingerprints without his permission?" I asked.

"Don't you ever watch *CSI*?"

The cop double-checked his tally and handed Kari the score sheet. "Guy got twelve right out of sixteen. Damn . . . damn!"

"Let me see the ones he missed," said Kari. She picked up the envelopes and opened them. "The Lieutenant at our party as the Jack the Ripper. And in this one, Merle's husband's wearing a Grim Reaper costume." Kari and I looked at each other. "Maybe if we'd used people's high school photos, he'd have gotten even more of them right."

I nodded. "I think he's for real. And he wants to help. What do you think?"

Kari rubbed the back of her neck. "I think I wanna talk to that boy about my stock investments."

That night I dreamt Trevor and I were dancing at a gay bar, having a good ole time. But when the music stopped, the scar erupted from his skin and turned into a snake—a nasty, violet-colored reptile that leapt out of his cheek and chased me. I woke up in a heart-thudding adrenaline rush and immediately checked under my bed.

30

HOOK, LINE, AND STINKER

The week the San Diego police ran Trevor's fingerprints through national crime databases, Dr. Winter released me to return to work part-time. In some ways I welcomed the routine and normalcy. Yet now that I had less free time, I grew more determined than ever to solve Belle Farby's murder. I worked Tuesday, Wednesday, and Thursday that week; Darlene invited me to go fishing with her on Friday. I'm all for Vatican II, but fish on Friday appealed.

I scooted the Silver Bullet in front of Darlene's home. She wanted to drive, so we loaded poles, an ice chest, and other gear into her Subaru, and cruised I-8 West toward Ocean Beach.

O.B. is the San Diego neighborhood in which Bob Marley would have felt most comfortable—plenty of beach to make sand angels, more co-op grocers than fast food chains, and more hashish than lattés. We exited the freeway and drove along palm-lined Sunset Cliffs Boulevard through the hippie beach community to the main drag, Newport Avenue. Its coffeehouses, tattoo parlors, fish taco joints, and head shops could all have been there when Joplin and Lennon rocked the planet. Only the body piercing services now offered on Newport might have raised unpierced eyebrows in their day.

Darlene maneuvered her Subaru into a tight spot in the parking lot at the foot of the O.B. pier. It's the longest concrete pier in the country—a Viking longboat of cement, bird droppings, and gray paint, set on pilings slick with algae. The place smelled like ylang ylang aromatherapy oil on saltines. Two seagulls tussled over a discarded burger on the roof of the bait and tackle shop as we hauled our gear toward the business end of the pier. It was one of those breezy days when, in my childhood, I would have listened to Ma's sheets snap on the clothesline.

Darlene and I moved companionably as we settled in. "Need some bait?" I asked.

She shook her head no, and began preparing her hook with something she'd brought in her cooler. She didn't offer me any.

I purchased a container of squid from the bait shop. I'd forgotten my bait knife when we transferred my gear to her car, so I figured I'd borrow hers when she was done using it. But I didn't have to wait for the knife; whatever she was using already came in such tiny pieces that she had to thread them on the hook with care.

If I don't catch anything, fishing bores me to tears. Instead of telling Darlene how bored I was, however, I regaled her with tales of my stay in the hospital. The facility where I underwent the mastectomy and reconstruction was a direct competitor of her employer. I, of course, teased that I got the best care anyone could want. She pretended not to react, but I noticed her color rise.

"You still OK about not opting for chemo or radiation?" she asked.

I nodded. "So far, anyway. That's been the hardest part: weighing quality of life against possible medical benefits, and making what I hope is a balanced decision." I reeled in my line, disgusted at its chewed off bait and empty hook. "Guess you health care workers are used to quality of life dilemmas. What'd you think of the Terry Schiavo case?"

"Muddy waters. Pisses me off when people expect doctors and nurses to have the answers. Trust me, the only person who knows how to make a quality of life decision is the person whose quality of life is threatened. Those wishes should be respected. No matter how crazy."

The topic seemed to irritate her, probably because it was work-related. I asked about her funniest Thanksgiving dinner story—we all have one—as I cast my line again. By the time she told me about her favorite grade school teacher and I'd told her why I like gin, I'd abandoned hope of catching anything. Darlene had nabbed two sculpin that she tossed back and was now reeling in a hefty queen fish.

I grew even more bored. I told Darlene about the psychic test and fingerprint tracking on Trevor. She listened attentively. "I wouldn't get my hopes up too high," I warned. "Trevor wants to help, but his ability isn't something he can produce on demand. He's willing to check the murder scene, but we don't even know where that is."

Darlene nodded and hauled in a 15-inch opal eye perch. I got my chance when she remembered she had to make a phone call. She walked a few feet away, snapped open her cell, and turned her back toward me. I lifted the lid of her bait cooler and peeked in. The tiny bait pieces were translucent with a brownish tinge, and smelled mighty rank. Jellyfish membranes? Whatever it was, the fish sure liked it. Maybe to Nemo's nose, freshly baked bread smells disgusting.

When she finished her call, she baited the treble hook on her line, unlocked her reel, and cast off. "We had a psychic as a patient at the hospital once," she shared. "She came in with a herniated disk and we did an MRI of her spine. Afterwards she claimed the magnetism in the MRI screwed up her psychic power; said her root chakra was buzzing. Got herself a lawyer and charged us with 'changing her charges'!"

We sat there laughing, our lines bobbing in the dark water below. Darlene began to sing. Between gusts of wind, I could just hear her voice lilting an old folk song, "Through streets broad and narrow crying 'Cockles and mussels! Alive, alive oh!'"

I turned toward her and for the first time that day, really studied her appearance. Her hair shone copper in the sunlight, though some was smooshed under her sun visor. The pain of losing Belle had added lines to her face. She'd lost some weight. Through her sandals, apricot-polished toenails beckoned. I found the dab of sunscreen on the bridge of her nose endearing.

I remembered Darlene said she met Belle when Belle was hospitalized for an appendectomy. If the price of meeting the right partner was paid in flesh, maybe now that I'd lost a breast, I'd find Ms. Right. It occurred to me there, on the pier, as a breeze burnished our cheeks, that a nurse might be the perfect match for me. A nurse probably wouldn't be repulsed by my incisions and scars. I watched my line for a moment, and joined her for the last verse. "She died of a fever/ And no one could save her/ And that was the end of sweet Molly Malone . . ." (Were those tears in Darlene's eyes?) ". . . But her ghost wheels the barrow/ Through streets broad and narrow/ Crying 'Cockles and mussels! Alive, alive oh!'"

As if on cue, Darlene spun her reel and landed another damn queen fish, this one larger than the first.

"OK, I can't stand it any more," I admitted. "What *is* that bait you're using?"

With complete deadpan, she answered, "Friend of mine works in Maternity. She gives me the foreskins of babies circumcised at birth. The fish love 'em."

I couldn't tell if she was blowing sunshine up my skirt or not, but those bright hazel eyes told me I would get no further explanation. I looked out across the breakers. "Gives a whole new meaning to 'cockles', doesn't it?"

31

IF I ONLY HAD
A BULGE

Stimulated by the time with Darlene, on the drive home my thoughts moved faster than a tweaker with an open credit line. A traffic light turned red. Red. Stop. Red. Passion. Why are 'stop' and 'passion' associated with the same color? Why stop passion? Stop pain, not passion. What stops pain? Healing? What heals? Whatever you believe in? Is healing mind over matter? Am I starting to believe in all this woo woo stuff? Twelve out of sixteen is beyond guesswork. How is it that Trevor 'knows' things that other people don't? Knows . . . nose. Damn, I miss the smell of a woman's hair on the pillow next to mine in the morning. I need to call Lee Anne.

Venus only knows at what platform this train of thought might have arrived if the street light hadn't turned green.

No "Good day!" from Raj greeted me when the Silver Bullet smooched our driveway. Nothing from Pookie either. I missed their friendly yelps.

Lana's truck was gone. Maybe she was treating the critters to play time at a park. Too bad; I was itching to regale her with the bait story. The sun warmed my shoulders and an air current set huge bird-of-paradise blossoms aquiver as I sauntered to the front door. I stretched my arms out wide to embrace the day, which pulled one of my incisions. Ouch. Sometimes my body gets cranky about all the cuts. I figure it has every right to.

The living room looked overtly normal, but something seemed off kilter. Barely detectable over my own eau de O.B. pier, I smelled something fruity. Mango? Peaches? It wasn't Lana's fragrance.

I called to Lana. No answer. I inspected my bedroom where I retrieved my .22. A thorough pass at Lana's room and the hall bath revealed nothing standing, sitting, sleeping, or slithering in that wing of the house.

I checked the dining room, sunporch, and kitchen. I glimpsed an empty Coors can in the kitchen trash. Lana and I put our empty aluminum cans in the recycling bin. Neither of us drinks Coors.

A sheet of notebook paper lay on the counter. In unfamiliar handwriting, the note ordered, *Lana, Urgent! Take the dogs and meet me at the San Ysidro border crossing. I'll find you down there. Will explain later. Tess.*

More interrogatives than explanations parsed into life's sentence. I could now guess where Lana and the dogs were, but who wrote the note? And after knowing me all these years, could she really believe that was my handwriting?

I calculated the cosines of danger. Someone obviously had been in our home. Someone obviously wanted the house empty. I heard the familiar ring of a cell phone. Could it be that special someone?

My own cell was silent; the sound originated from somewhere in the backyard. I drew my gun, unlocked its safety, and slid open the patio door. A garnet-chested hummingbird beat its way into view near our feeder. Other than its winged busy-ness, all seemed peaceful on the patio. The ringing stopped. I didn't hear anyone talking. Cautiously, I ventured into the backyard and nearly dropped the gun in surprise.

In the middle of Lana's herb garden stood a scarecrow. The head was a plastic Halloween pumpkin. The straw body overflowed its denim jeans and red T-shirt. Atop the shiny orange head sat a Padres ball cap, and rubber bands held cheap costume boots in place. Unfazed by the "scare" in scarecrow, a starling perched on one of the outstretched arms. No matter how hard I scrutinized, the scarecrow did not appear to be carrying a cell phone. My attention was drawn, however, to one particular part of its anatomy.

In 1971, the Rolling Stones released an album called *Sticky Fingers*. Its cover art featured a man's denim-clad pelvic area with a sizable lump under the zipper. Parents hated the album. Viagra should've bought rights. The scarecrow appeared as well endowed as the *Sticky Fingers* dude.

After exploring the entire backyard, I reset the gun's safety, and ventured to within a few feet of the straw and stick man. I stared. I could hardly avoid staring. Was that a munchkin in his pocket or was he just glad to see Dorothy?

Though full of tumescence, the scarecrow seemed benign. My curiosity grew bolder until it finally rolled sevens and won. I reached out. The bulge felt warm to the touch, which made sense, since the figure had been standing, unshaded, in afternoon sun. I pressed gently. Firm but yielding . . . hmm. I started to unzip the fly. When the zipper was down about three inches, the head of a snake popped out.

An ancient fear flooded my brain, jittered my limbs, zigzagged through my belly, and nearly reached my sphincter. This time, curiosity had rolled snake eyes.

The snake didn't move, and in fact, looked dead, but I took no chances. I rezipped the jeans and tore back into the house. I no longer gave a damn about finding the cell phone or its owner in the backyard; I just wanted to put distance between me and the scarecrow. I don't even think I exhaled until I'd closed the back door behind me.

The knot in my stomach unraveled when I saw Lana come through the front door a few minutes later. I'd been so distracted I'd hardly realized how anxious I was for her safety. Friendly barks and doggy kisses abounded, but almost immediately Raj sniffed his way to the scarecrow. I took Lana by the arm and we followed him. He let out a few yips, but otherwise seemed calm for such a good watchdog.

Lana glanced at the scarecrow without looking closely, bent down, and began resuscitating the trodden herb leaves near it. Her usually velvet voice was embroidered with peeve. "Why didn't you ask me first before you put this up?"

I didn't respond. When she stood up, Lana's exotic eyes caught the bulge in the pants, then took a round trip back toward me. If I'd had the camera, I would've snapped that expression.

"Don't touch it—there's a snake in there!" Anticipating her next question, I added, "I think it's dead. I've already called the cops." We walked back in the house. Lana steeped a cup of Sutra Strength tea and offered me one.

"No, thanks. Finding a *real* trouser snake calls for something 'stiff,' if you'll pardon the expression." I emptied a bottle of Bombay Sapphire into a glass and added ice. "Why did you go?" I asked her. "You had to know that wasn't my handwriting on the note."

"Of course I knew," she admitted. Her lips trembled slightly as she sipped her spicy tea. "The handwriting on the note was legible." She offered a fleeting grin at the expense of my penmanship. "When I came home from class, I felt a negative aura in the house; then I saw the note. I thought you were in trouble and needed help, so I drove to San Ysidro to check things out. When no one showed up, I came home."

In gratitude for her muddle-headed but well-intentioned trip to the border, I hugged her.

She quickly pulled back. "You smell fishy!"

When I returned from sorely needed ablutions, I filled her in on what little I knew about the situation. When the doorbell rang, I damned near had to dance a tarantella to maneuver around Pookie. Gratefully, I invited Kari in.

Kari nodded at Lana with a blend of courtesy and condescension, turned back toward me and asked, "You OK? What's going on? I got some crazy message about a prowler and a scarecrow?"

"Come see for yourself." I turned toward the back door.

"Where're we headed?"

Linnaeus would have frowned at its technical inaccuracy, but I couldn't resist. "We're off to see the lizard!"

32

SHRUGGED, UNPLUGGED, AND BUGGED

"The mere presence of a rattlesnake in someone's backyard hardly incriminates my client." Mongoose Matthews's attorney, Mark Fanuel, seemed competent and confident.

Ninety-three degree heat was nearly unheard of in early December, when Mongoose's preliminary hearing took place. But either global warming or Santa Ana winds mocked the calendar. The air conditioning system sputtered petulantly through vents in the ceiling of Room 2016, on the second floor of the San Diego County Superior Court building. Lana and I sat in hard plastic chairs in the windowless room, surrounded by too much cheap wood paneling. Lana fanned herself with a newsletter she'd found in her purse.

Myrna Ryder, an assistant D.A., resembled a dinner roll but spoke like cayenne pepper. She jammed her glasses against the bridge of her nose and shot her words. "Your Honor, the Mojave rattler is rare in San Diego County, *except* in the Borrego Springs area where the accused resides."

Matthews's mouthpiece weighed in. "My client is hardly the only resident of—"

The judge brought the gavel down lightly and loosened the collar of his robe. "Excuse me. Bailiff, see if we can get another fan in this courtroom. It must be over 90 degrees in here." The bailiff exited in search of cooling devices, and the judge returned to business. "Sorry, Mr. Fanuel. You were saying?"

"Mr. Matthews is only one of approximately 3,000 residents of Borrego Springs. The fact that a certain type of snake was found on Ms. Camillo's property holds no particular significance for my client."

The bailiff entered through the back of the courtroom carrying the most decrepit electrical fan I'd ever seen. I'm no expert on appliance evolution, but it appeared to be from the Maltese Falcon era. Its cord was badly frayed. I flinched when the bailiff plugged it in, certain I was about to witness an electrocution sans conviction. But the fan didn't spark or sputter. In fact, nothing happened, period. The bailiff shrugged, unplugged, perspired, and retreated.

Ryder sprang to her feet. "Not only can Mojave rattlesnakes be found near Mr. Matthews's home, but the defendant *works* with rattlesnakes. He would be one of very few people who could handle such an animal. Mr. Matthews was arrested for a felony rape—"

"And found not guilty," Fanuel interjected.

Ryder lost no momentum. "Due to a technicality. And he was once under FBI investigation for attempting to intimidate certain people by placing snake skins in their mailbo—"

"A charge dropped for lack of evidence," Fanuel clarified.

In the midst of this legal seesaw, I sensed someone staring at me. I scanned the courtroom until my eyes locked with Mongoose Matthews's reckless blue ones. He recognized me but seemed confused by my presence in the courtroom. After apparently considering all approaches, he licked his lips salaciously with his tongue. What he lacked in subtlety, he made up for in saliva. I refocused on the one-upmanship of lawyers.

"….retrieved from the property?"

"Yes, your Honor. From the trashcan in the kitchen. The fingerprints were a twelvepoint match."

With the regularity of a bear in the woods on a high-fiber diet, Matthews's attorney counterattacked. "Judge, my client disposes of aluminum cans in a recycling bin along the public road in front of his house. Anyone could have removed one and placed it at the Camillo property. Besides, witnesses can establish my client's whereabouts at the time of the crime."

"And where exactly was he, Mr. Fanuel?" the judge inquired.

We waited in suspense for the answer because the bailiff returned at that moment carrying a small cardboard box. He approached the judge and showed him the contents. The judge did not seem pleased.

The bailiff hung his head. "It's the best I could do on short notice."

The judge reached into the box, picked out a small battery-operated handheld fan and turned it on. It whirred, but offered ridiculously little cooling.

Mongoose whispered in his attorney's ear. Fanuel spoke

to the judge. "If it pleases the court, my client says he has experience fixing air conditioning units. If your Honor will indulge us with a brief recess, Mr. Matthews will attempt to repair the air conditioner. Without compensation."

The judge smacked the gavel once. "By all means. It's sweltering in here. Bailiff, find some tools for Mr. Matthews. Guard, escort the defendant down the corridor to the air conditioning unit and supervise him while he works. Court will reconvene in one hour."

By the time we returned, the temperature in the courtroom was approaching tolerable. I guess even Mongoose Matthews has redeeming qualities.

The judge resumed the hearing. "Mr. Fanuel, before the recess you were saying there are witnesses to your client's whereabouts at the time of the crime?"

"Yes, your Honor. These gentlemen," Fanuel indicated three scruffy fellows in their late twenties sitting together, "helped my client repair the crankshaft of his truck on the afternoon in question. Mr. Johnson and Mr. Talbott are prepared to testify they arrived at my client's home around 2:30 P.M. Mr. Cade, about 3:15. At 4:30, all of them rode together to Ali's Auto Parts. Employees of the parts store will testify to that. The men returned to my client's home where they continued to work on the vehicle until about 6:00 P.M., at which time they went out socializing together."

Translation: When they ran out of six-packs in the garage, they went to a bar and got tanked. By either version, Matthews had an alibi.

It didn't take the judge long to show his appreciation for the air conditioning. He looked at the three punks. "Are you gentlemen prepared to so testify?"

"Yup."

"No problem."

"Yes, your Highness."

The judge blinked once when recognized as royalty, but did not falter long. "The District Attorney's office has presented insufficient evidence to send this case to trial. Mr. Matthews is released from custody."

The gavel cracked and so did Lana's nerves. She turned to me in tears. "They're letting him go!"

"C'mon, let's go home." I put my arm around her shoulders. I wasn't feeling all that comfortable either, with a skewed soul like Matthews wandering the streets. We rode the steep escalator down to the first floor and scraped our feet on parking lot gravel as we walked to the car. I slid a Sheryl Crow CD into the stereo and hoped the music would bolster both of us. As I drove north on First Avenue through Hillcrest, I told her, "For what it's worth, I don't think Mongoose put the scarecrow in our yard."

"You believe his alibi?"

"I don't know if the alibi's true or not." I pulled the car into the driveway, this time enjoying the friendly yips of Raj and Pookie. "But other things make me think he didn't do it."

It wasn't until we were sitting in our breakfast nook with tea and ginger beer to soothe our frazzled nerves, that I elaborated. "That day I visited Matthews, he got pissed off and threatened me with a knife."

"The same day he kissed you? Tess, you never told me." Lana began.

"It's what he *didn't* do that's interesting. He had a garage full of rattlesnakes, but he never threatened me with them.

When he got aggressive, he grabbed a knife. He also used a knife in the rape he committed." With my napkin I blotted the condensation ring my ginger beer left on the table. "Whoever this Rattler Man is, he's been careful not to leave any evidence behind. Not a trace at Darlene's house when he attacked her. Not a trace when we found the king snake in our sunporch. Now suddenly, he leaves behind a Coors can? I don't think so. Mongoose Matthews is a venereal wart, but he's not our Rattler Man, Lana. Someone's setting him up."

Lana pondered that as she gazed out the kitchen window. Suddenly, ex nihilo, she announced, "I have to go fly a kite!" And zoom, she was out of her chair, heading for the door, Pookie and Raj nipping at her heels in excitement.

"We're in deep discussion here, and suddenly you need to fly a kite?"

"Just remembered—I promised one of my Tai Chi students I'd teach her five-year-old how to fly a kite today. I was supposed to meet them at Fiesta Island at two." We both glanced at the kitchen clock. It was 2:19. Lana continued, "If I hurry, I shouldn't be too late."

Only Lana could leave that late for an appointment and still not be "too late." I felt a bit jealous; I'd rather go fly a kite, too, especially in these Santa Ana winds, but this whole snake business was starting to crawl up my kite string. I decided to catch up on e-mails, eager for anything new Roark had finagled on Belle's murder.

I wasn't disappointed. A political cartoon from Tiger. A link to "vicarious memes" that Celeste suggested I explore. And the current police report on the investigation of the scarecrow incident. Once again, it astonished me how little physical evidence was left behind. The scarecrow's clothing had been traced to a Salvation Army thrift store with no surveillance cameras. The plastic pumpkin head and costume boots had been purchased, in cash, at a Target in the San Diego area last Halloween, but it was impossible to tell by whom. Except on the Coors can, there were no unfamiliar fingerprints anywhere. Rattler Man had apparently kept to his modus operandi of wearing gloves. Hay, probably grown and sold locally, was the source of the scarecrow straw, but that offered no clues. The handwriting on the note left for Lana might prove useful eventually, if we ever had a suspect's handwriting with which to compare it. Rattler Man left less impact on his physical environment than the ghost of an albino daddy longlegs.

One other e-mail spun my bottle. The breast cancer portal site had referred my inquiry about snake venom research to a professor at USC School of Medicine who'd found a venom protein that slowed breast and ovarian cancer cell growth in mice. The professor e-mailed that the protein was still being probed, and other venom-based breast cancer research was being conducted right at UCSD, the campus where Belle's body was discovered. I logged onto the UCSD site. Snakes used in the research project were housed in space subcontracted from the hospital where Darlene worked.

I wondered. As surely as Lana would go fly a kite—as surely as Pookie would fall for the Door Trick—as surely as I had lost a breast—and as surely as some perverse jokester hid a snake in a scarecrow's jockstrap—I wondered.

With ideas buzzing the back forty of my brain, I rose quickly and started toward the living room. My shoulder accidentally caught my dresser scarf and something fell to the floor. I bent over to pick it up. It was one of the kitschy earrings Trevor had given me. Its plastic exterior had broken in half, revealing a tiny microphone transmitter. We'd been bugged.

33

VISIONS OF
THE GREAT GODDESS

I was at work, cleaning lint from my mouse's navel, when the call came through.

"Just standard Radio Shack equipment," Kari declared. "Trevor's no Secret Agent Man."

Bigger-than-Rolaids relief. Ever since I'd found the transmitter the night before, I'd worried that some national security überseer had detected Roark's cyber-bean spilling. I didn't want my ex to lose his job when he'd only been trying to help. Curiosity soon conquered relief. "If Trevor's not a spy, why was he bugging my home?"

"To learn something he could use to dazzle you with the accuracy of his psychic ability, so you would persuade us to use him in the Belle Farby murder investigation. Least that's what he says." Kari let that register, and continued. "Says he felt he could help, but was afraid dealing with us cop types would only bring him ridicule. His psychic revelations told him to go to you. So he bugged your place."

"To get inside info that would convince me he was legit?" I recalled my astonishment in the police station when he warned me I could rupture my stitches by playing hard with the dogs. "So in turn I'd push you guys to use him?"

"That's his story and he's stickin' to it."

The sharp end of the straightened paper clip I'd wedged into my mouse missed its target. I palmed the phone receiver and whispered, "Walker, this thing belongs in an antiquities museum."

"Sorry?" Kari heard too much but not enough.

"My bad," I apologized as Walker ducked into his office. I tuned back into Kari. "Look, I don't think Trevor's story would sell on the boardwalk, if you know what I mean. But the story doesn't matter; he's going to prison for Belle's murder, right?"

"Murder? No way. We got nothing on him, other than invasion of your privacy."

Lana might have a meltdown if she knew Mongoose *and* Trevor were out walking the streets. "He knew details about Belle Farby's murder that no one but the murderer could know."

"Remember the psychic test we gave him? Right in downtown police headquarters, this guy *proved* he gets reception on wavelengths the rest of us don't hear." She paused. "Girl, it doesn't matter what I suspect; it doesn't matter what you suspect; it only matters what the evidence proves."

"Didn't I hear that on *Law & Order* the other night?"

"Smart ass. Anyway, we only have evidence that he invaded your privacy. *If* you want to press charges."

"If? Why wouldn't I?"

"Don't pop your garters, Tess, but I kinda like the guy. I know he's strange, but I don't read him as a violent perp. Ever since he took that psychic test and I realized he was family and he wasn't just a con artist, I don't know . . . His prints weren't in NCIC; he's got no priors. Besides, there's no reason to think he knows jack about poisonous snakes."

"All right, I won't press charges, not now, anyway. Can you get a handwriting sample to compare against the note left in our house?"

"Got one before he lawyered up. It's on its way to the graphology center for analysis. Got a few more things I can check out. We'll tie him up with paperwork for a while." Call-waiting signaled its presence on her line. "I'll keep you posted. Gotta go."

The good thing about programming for the Web these days was that I had a universe of information at the tip of the nose of my antiquated mouse, and Walker would be hard-put to tell whether my efforts were work-related or recreational. The downside was that employers were figuring out it cost less to pay programmers in New Delhi or Lagos than it did to pay U.S. programmers. Since my diagnosis, rumors abounded that the days of Imitech's charitable foundation were numbered. Two admin types and one Flash animator had already been laid off. My abridged work schedule made me acutely vulnerable to a lay-off. I promptly returned to writing intricate if/then statements.

At least I had something fun to look forward to after work. Lana had a hot date with Nate, but Celeste, Tiger, and I were hooking up for a special lecture at the San Diego Museum of Art on Visions of the Great Goddess. The day we made the plans, I told them my current life held too few nipples, curves, and lips, and I was reasonably sure a few of the goddess visions would manifest them. Celeste said no one could possibly be as politically incorrect as I pretend to be, and Tiger (who's known me longer) hoped some day they'd offer Visions of Hunky Gods as well.

After work, I scrunched the Silver Bullet into a tight parking space near the organ pavilion in Balboa Park. I was early, and decided to stroll through the park's giant eucalyptus trees. Their slender leaves shimmered silver and olive green in the late afternoon sun, while their cough drop scent mingled with the smell of fresh popcorn from a sidewalk vendor. Ever since the vendors started putting that toxic orange slime-oil on popcorn instead of real butter, popcorn smells different than it did when we were kids. Of course, *we* smell different than when we were kids, too, which may be a good thing.

As I walked, images related to Belle Farby's murder played on my mind like a PowerPoint with no End Show function. Over and over they flashed: a pleasant looking woman laid out on palm fronds along the UCSD Snake Path, hairs and buttons dappling her shirt, and two fang marks on her neck. Family and friends weeping under the gazebo at the memorial service. A coiled snake tattooed on Arlo George's forearm. Darlene, soiled by her own spew, struggling against the effects of rattlesnake venom. Mongoose Matthews stroking the venom glands of "Frankies" as he milked them. The alarming bulge in a scarecrow's jeans.

How did Trevor the psychic fit into all of this? Was he involved in the murder? Raj hadn't barked at Trevor when he met him, as though he sensed Trevor held no threat. I remembered the vulnerability conveyed by Trevor's facial scar and how he nearly puked at the police station over the Sally Debonnes case. Maybe the guy really was just trying to help. I'd know more when his handwriting sample was analyzed.

I stepped out of the eucalyptus grove and headed toward the San Diego Art Museum. Adjacent to the museum's parking lot gurgles a fountain, jets of water arcing gracefully before emptying into a cistern. The fountain is trimmed in Mexican tiles. I checked my watch: 4:35 P.M. Celeste and Tiger would be here shortly. I decided the fountain was a fine place to wait; so did two squirrels and a homeless fellow. Nearby, a work crew dismantled signs mounted expressly for "Christmas in the Prado," and replaced them with poinsettias and colored tree lights.

As I sat there pondering Belle's murder, I recognized a woman walking toward me from the direction of the natural history museum, about a block away. She was holding hands with a well-dressed, dark-haired guy of average height.

The man kissed her and departed in the direction of the zoo. As Susan Duffy, the one suspect who definitely knew her way around snakes, approached, her downward gaze made eye contact impossible. When I greeted her, she nearly escaped her epidermis.

"Hi! It's Tess Camillo. Remember me?" She still had the air of someone whose personal pinball machine was permanently on tilt, but she did seem a tad more attractive. Was that lipstick she was wearing? And blush? Even the lube sheen on her hair looked mildly diminished.

When she finally made eye contact, the weak eye assured me it really was her. I threw caution over the Laurel Street Bridge and asked, "Who was that guy I just saw you with?"

Rigidity entered her posture. "A friend." She continued to walk and I fell in beside her.

We dodged a Hispanic woman with a stroller of wailing twins. "Must be your boyfriend. I mean, he kissed you." She failed to acknowledge the implied question. Maybe I needed a less direct approach. "How have you been? Getting ready for Christmas?"

She mumbled something that may have indicated an affirmative in a galaxy far, far away. She glanced back toward the man who was now nearly out of sight, headed toward the zoo parking lot. The San Diego Zoo—home of koalas, gorillas, rhinos, pandas, and at least one *Oxyuranus microlepidotus*—reminded me that the only person who'd voluntarily quit a job lately was Susan Duffy. She'd left her position at the zoo, an institution some folks waited years to get into. Though the police had interrogated her about it, and I'd asked her when we met, no one had yet gotten a straight answer. As we walked, I told her about my bout with breast cancer. No matter how spacey or strange the female, that subject connects.

"Are you all right now?" she asked kindly.

"So they tell me." We walked silently for a moment. "Susan, you worked at the zoo, didn't you?"

"Um hmm."

"Zoo jobs are coveted positions. Whatever made you leave?"

She stopped and turned toward me. "The guy you saw me with? Sean Taylor. We've dated off and on for years. In late September, Sean was offered a job at the zoo. In my department, herpetology."

As if I could forget. That musky reptilian smell still pervaded her clothes.

She continued. "Zoo policies discourage employees from getting, uh, romantically," her tongue nearly refused to pronounce the word, "involved with people in the same division."

"You gave up your job so Sean could accept one?" This guy must wear Cobra aftershave.

"Maybe it wasn't . . . never mind. You didn't want to date me when I admitted I was bisexual. You probably think bisexuality is messed up."

"It may not be my thing, but if being bisexual is who you really are, if it's what you really want, go for it." I attempted to boost her flagging, or perhaps gagging, spirits.

She sighed and the sound came from a place where despair never goes on vacation. "Truth is, I don't care whether I date men. Or women. I don't really care if I date at all."

We arrived at her car. She slid her key in the door lock.

"You don't know me well, and you probably trust me less," I said, "but talking to a therapist might help." I turned from her Visage of Great Sadness, and prepared for Visions of the Great Goddess.

34

HOPI TALES TO YOU

On the drive home, one of the most beautiful mathematical phenomena popped into my mind: Euler's number, or "e" in his honor. A college professor taught us about Euler's Formula, which uses Euler's number, by singing to the tune of Don McLean's "American Pie":

> *A long, long time ago,*
> *A mathematician found out how complexes*
>   *exponentiate*
> *And now if you've got some time*
> *I will try to do in rhyme*
> *A proof of this theorem great . . .*

The chorus went:

> *i times the sine of the y*
> *(comes from Taylor's; tell you later how all*
>   *this came by)*

To that you add the cosine of y
Equals e taken to i y;
Equals e taken to i y . . .

The mind can be a contentious mule, utterly refusing to traverse the fertile field you want to plow, yet hauling significant burdens uphill to access a destination of its own choosing. What brought Euler's number to my mule of a mind? Usually hearing the Don McLean song triggers it, but I hadn't heard "American Pie" recently. I finally realized that Susan Duffy's friend was Sean *Taylor*, and the chorus referred to *Taylor*'s number series. My subconscious must have linked the two. A normal brain would have linked to Elizabeth Taylor, or to a tailor. But no one has yet accused me of normalcy.

I was about to turn on the car stereo to rid myself of the addictive tune when Kari called my cell phone.

"Got some news, girl." She sounded somber. "Can you swing by the station?"

"This late? I will if you need me to, but I'm bone tired." The surgery had reduced my stamina more than I liked to admit. After a day's work, the walk in Balboa Park, an art lecture, and a drink with Celeste and Tiger, I was beat.

"No, you don't really need to. Guess I'm just stalling."

In case she was going to announce another murder, I pulled over and parked along palm-lined Sixth Avenue, bordering the park. Overhead palm branches smudged the purplish night sky. I listened as Kari explained, "Trevor Tribeca's real name is Sean Trevor. We found records on him. Guess who he's connected with?"

Headlights of an oncoming car strobed through the Silver Bullet. I felt exposed. A car I didn't recognize pulled up behind me. My pulse took up jogging. "You'd better just tell me," I answered Kari.

"Sean Trevor, the psychic we know as Trevor Tribeca, lived in Pensacola, Florida, twenty-two years ago, where his parents filed assault charges against one Wade 'Mongoose' Matthews for slicing up Trevor's face with a knife."

The driver behind me honked his horn. Apparently he'd spotted my car with the lights on and me in the driver's seat, and decided I must be ready to vacate my parking space. I waved him on. He ignored me. "So Mongoose Matthews gave Trevor that scar?"

"Looks that way." I could hear her sliding file drawers. "When we couldn't find his prints in the national crime database, we decided just for thoroughness, to subpoena any sealed juvenile records. Files arrived this afternoon. Matthews was sixteen, Trevor, thirteen, at the time."

"How did it happen?" I inquired.

"Matthews accused Trevor of coming on to him. Matthews felt the insult to his teen machismo justified pulling a knife."

"And using it."

"Got that right," Kari agreed. "And you know how gay boys are about their looks. Matthews gave Trevor a nasty-ass facial scar he's carried for a lot of years."

"This means Trevor had a motive for setting up Matthews as our Rattler Man."

I could almost see Kari worrying her dreadlocks, chagrined by her charitable defense of Trevor earlier in the day. "It explains a lot."

"Except the most important thing: why Trevor—or any-one—killed Belle Farby." I paused. "Kari, was Trevor still in custody at the station around 4:30, 4:45 this afternoon?" I asked, remembering Susan Duffy's boyfriend.

"No. When you said you weren't going to press charges for invading your privacy, we sprung him. Must've been around three o'clock."

"I ran into Susan Duffy late this afternoon in Balboa Park. She was with a guy named Sean Taylor. I only caught a glimpse of him. He's got the same coloring as Trevor and he's about the same size. Sean Taylor; Sean Trevor?" The driver waiting for my parking spot blasted his horn again. "We know Trevor uses pseudonyms; maybe he's got multiple identities. Duffy said her boyfriend was a herpetologist. That's a day job. He could still work the evening shift for a psychic phone line."

"I'm on it. Later."

I was happy to vacate the parking space for Mr. Rude, just to end his honking. I agreed with Kari's earlier assessment; Trevor didn't feel like a violent perp. He seemed kind and vulnerable, as though the facial scar reflected only the surface of his woundedness. But what if his emotional wounds had festered? What if he was, indeed, our Rattler Man?

When I arrived home, Lana's rust heap was parked in front of the house behind Nate the soccer player's BMW M3 coupe.

Now that I've gotten over the worst of the best love affair I've ever had, I rather like it when Lana or I bring home a date. When she eventually finds the man of her drawers, and or I find the woman of my wrist cuffs, it'll hurt—hugely—to go our separate ways. But in the meantime, dating provides stimulation, and at least the house gets cleaned when we bring someone home. Enough time had lapsed since Nate and Lana's last encounter for dust bunnies to accumulate along the baseboards.

Though exhausted, if I went to bed now, their mattress marathon would keep me awake, so I crashed on the living room sofa. Raj laid his sweet muzzle on my belly and I stroked his head. Pookie, lowly dachshund that she is, couldn't reach high enough to annoy me. I heard a particularly acute moan coming from the hallway and smiled.

Our relationship may not be easy to categorize by the Dewey decimal system, but I love Lana deeply. Her happiness makes me happy. Love stretches, distorts, bothers, and bewilders the heart, changing us in ways we least expect.

I scratched Raj in a special spot, near his left ear. I know it's not possible, but I thought I heard him purr. My eyes wandered to the colorful cover of Lana's textbook she'd left nearby on the end table. I picked it up, skimmed a few paragraphs on Navaho fry bread, and dozed off.

I dreamt I saw Darlene on the O.B. pier, talking on her cell about the number of queen fish she'd caught. A boom box was playing nearby, and she tried to turn down its volume. A scarecrow yanked the radio from her hands and put its straw ear to the speaker. When it raised its head, a map of Florida was burned into its straw cheek. Darlene retrieved one of her piscine trophies and laid the fish across my stomach. The sensation of wet fish scales on my belly was so powerful, I woke up.

Raj's tongue was licking my tummy. Not exactly the

same level of tongue action Lana was probably experiencing, but hey, I'll take what I can get.

The house was now quiet; time to head for my own sheets. I stirred. Lana's book, which had fallen across my chest, slid to the floor. I picked it up. The book had opened to a photo of the Hopi Snake Dance. Hopi dancers, in a frenzy of rhythm and religious fervor, grasped rattlesnakes. Some wore them entwined around their necks. The power of belief can be stunning, especially in some of its stranger applications.

A moment later, a smile got on at my toes, rode past my pelvis and women's lingerie, skipped my mastectomied mezzanine, and arrived at my face. I replaced the book on the end table. I now knew who had killed Belle Farby. I knew most of the how. I might even know the sine of the Y. Tomorrow, I'd dig into the wherefores.

35

I GET THE POINT

The next morning, I noticed the toilet seat was up. "Did you do that, Raj?" I asked as I converted java beans into morning greetings. Raj took offense and denied any complicity in the episode. Nate's ride was still parked outside, so I gave Raj the benefit of the doubt.

I spread peanut butter on slices of a Gala apple and munched while I ruminated. Was my solution to Belle's murder as clear as it seemed last night? I slipped my plate and cup into the dishwasher, and headed for my computer.

I reviewed everything Roark had sent on the murder over the past few months. I also spent time researching a few things on the Web. If I was now correct about the murderer, we had been looking at this all wrong, all along.

I grew restless; I needed to think. Tinker Toys help me process, so I tossed mine on my bed and tried to construct the same mega-figure the five-year-old pictured on the Tinker Toys carton had apparently managed. Don't believe it: I tried for half an hour, and never achieved that exact zigzag effect.

I showered and dressed in blue jeans (reliable garb for any endeavor), an old purple blouse nubby with wear, and socks that used to be purple and were now the color that Fruit Loops turn milk.

I'd cruised half a block in the Silver Bullet when I dialed Kari on my cell. The call was routed to her voice mail. "Kari, I think I know who killed Belle Farby. I'm going to check something this morning, see if my theory's correct. If it is, I'll get back to you right away. Talk to you lat—oh, almost forgot—Trevor's handwriting will match the note from our house. But if you don't already have him back in custody, don't bother. I don't think he murdered anybody."

I zigzagged through the Mission Hills neighborhood in roughly the same pattern as the Tinker Toy construct, and parked my shiny wheels half a block from my destination. Before I stepped out, I grabbed the button securing the belly of my blouse and yanked it off.

It was 10:09 A.M.. Darlene wore beige denims, an aqua turtleneck, and house slippers when she answered the door. Her hair hinted of bed-head. I heard coffee percolating in the background and smelled its rich aroma. "For those of us who work an evening shift, it's a little early for a social visit, Tess." Her attitude prickled with briars of caution.

"Sorry to stop by unannounced," I began. "But my grandmother's coming for a visit. Her flight arrives in about forty minutes." I glanced pointedly at my watch. "I was only a block from here, on my way to pick her up at the airport, when I noticed I'd popped a button." I indicated the part of my shirt playing show-and-tell. "Figured if I could borrow your sewing kit, I wouldn't have to backtrack all the way home."

What did that flicker in those spirited hazel eyes mean? "Come on in. I'll get my sewing basket." She headed down the hall. I heard her fumbling through a closet.

The front door of Darlene's house opened into the middle of a cramped living room, with just enough space for a plaid couch along one wall, and two overstuffed armchairs—one blue, one red—along the other wall, with a TV stand between the chairs. Opposite the front door was an arched entranceway into the kitchen, where a side door opened from the garage. A coffee table sat in front of the couch, and that's where Darlene placed the sewing basket when she returned.

"Take off your blouse. I'll do it," she commanded.

I didn't much like that idea. Mastectomies lend modesty even to the brash and the passionate. Besides, being half undressed would make me vulnerable in a situation where I needed leverage. But what could I say? Darlene had accepted my harebrained story and was willing to help. She noticed my hesitation.

"Tess, I'm a nurse. There's not much I haven't seen in the way of human anatomy," she reassured.

I slipped off my blouse and sank into the couch, shoulders protectively hunched around my scarred torso. For once, I was grateful for my bra.

Darlene examined the blouse. "Got the button?" she inquired.

I shook my head no. "Lost it in the car somewhere." In as calm a voice as I could manage I asked, "Can we use one of yours?"

Darlene flashed a disturbed glare, but fished a small plastic box from the sewing basket. It contained eight shiny new buttons. Not a single old one. I was now pretty certain I knew where the old buttons had gone—all over Belle's corpse. She handed me the box.

I selected one of the new buttons and handed it to her. "This'll work."

When I looked up, she was holding a long sewing needle, poking thread through its eye. The needle image sent a shiver up my spine. Darlene caught my expression.

"Where's your grandmother coming from?" she asked.

"Little place called Bolivar, New York," I replied, choosing the hometown of a college fling. I no longer had a living grandmother, so it made more sense than saying she was flying in from Beyond the Sunset.

"Is that near Albany? Rochester?"

"Not near much of anything, really." I paused. "You were raised in a remote area, too, weren't you?" Darlene looked at me with surprise. "When you were packing things from your house in Point Loma, I saw your high school yearbook. Little town in Tennessee, right?"

She nodded. The sewing needle flew faster.

"That hymn you sang at Belle's funeral . . . it was so beautiful and heartfelt. "Amazing Grace" is the one I usually hear at funerals. The hymn you sang was unique. It had a primitive bluegrass feel to it. That kind of music usually originates in hill country." I shifted my weight on the couch. God, I wish I had my blouse on. "Those rural back pockets produce lots of interesting things."

Darlene gave me a peculiar look and reached toward her waist. "I'm on call today, Tess," she said, "and my cell phone just vibrated. Excuse me for a minute." She walked down the hall, taking my blouse with her.

I watched motes of dust float and sparkle in the morning light as I waited for Darlene to return. When she did, her demeanor had changed. My mended blouse was draped low over her right arm, covering her hand. She seemed to be grasping something, but I couldn't see what.

Inquisitiveness challenged prudence. It was probably time for me to exit, stage-left-behind-and-don't-look-back. I stood up. "Well, I gotta get to the airport. Thanks for the button." I moved toward her and reached for my blouse.

Darlene pulled back before I could grab it and walked over to the blue armchair. "I don't think there's a grandmother arriving at Lindbergh Field, Tess."

Involuntarily, I cast my eyes down in embarrassment.

Darlene's body tensed and her fair coloring flushed. In a stressed voice she asked, "How did you know?"

"In a book, I saw a picture of the Hopi Snake Dance—people carrying snakes in the name of the Great Spirit. It reminded me that, tucked in the hills of Appalachia, there are snake handling cults." I tried to figure out what was in her hand, under my blouse, as I spoke. "One of the biggest was in the Tennessee region where you grew up. I looked it up on the Web this morning. That's how you could take venomous snakes from the research lab in your hospital without getting bitten."

"Why couldn't you leave it alone?" Darlene kicked a wastebasket across the room. Must've hurt through the slippers. "Why couldn't you just leave it the hell alone?"

"There was a snake in my house last August, remember? I've had a vested interest in figuring out what was going on."

"That stupid rattler!" Her natural fire was stoked. "That was sheer coincidence."

"I finally accepted that," I admitted. I shook my head in puzzlement. "Why kill the woman you loved—and I believe you did love her—just when she really needed you? Were you afraid you couldn't cope?"

Darlene's glare stung me to the core. Two bright red spots flushed on either side of her neck. "You think I *wanted* to? I hated the idea, but Belle could be so stubborn. She insisted!" Tears welled in her eyes but her body language broadcast menace.

"Tell me what happened," I coaxed, and again tried to discern the nature of the object beneath the blouse.

"You know about the Huntington's?" Darlene asked.

I nodded. The post-mortem revealed a brain abnormality, a more spacious lateral ventricle indicating a loss of basal ganglial cells—an early sign of Huntington's. Neither the M.E. nor the police had caught the significance, nor would I, if I hadn't suspected the diagnosis and e-mailed Huntington's experts for verification.

Darlene stopped pacing near the other armchair and leaned against it. "We knew it was genetically linked, and she'd had mild symptoms. But we were so busy taking care of her father, Milt, I think we both were in denial. Anyway, as her own muscle spasms grew more frequent, Belle concocted this plan."

Darlene glanced down at whatever was in her hand. I took advantage of the momentary distraction to make another grab for my blouse. As the nubby purple cotton lifted from her arm, a long loaded hypodermic came into view. Shit. I would have been less intimidated by a machete, and she knew it.

Rapidly my skin grew chill and clammy and perspiration dotted my brow. I looked at Darlene. Her eyes connected with mine. She nodded toward my blouse. "You got it; might as well put it on."

My curiosity competed with my squeamishness over the shining metal pricker. I slipped an arm into one sleeve and I asked, "So this whole idea was Belle's?"

Darlene struggled with the words. "She didn't want to be a burden. There's no cure, you know; not much that can be done. We watched Milt suffer horribly." She started pacing.

I felt woozy each time she and that needle drew near but managed to get my blouse buttoned.

Darlene offered more. "I told her I didn't mind caring for her; we'd been through thick and thin together. Besides, I'm a nurse, who better suited?" She fought back tears. "Tell me, Tess . . . tell me . . . What the hell was I supposed to do when the woman I love . . . have loved my whole life . . . asks me to *kill* her?" When she regained some control, she continued. "Most forms of euthanasia would immediately point to me, because of my access to drugs." She lifted the needle as though she were toasting with bubbly.

A things-are-definitely-not-right queasiness caught the B train through my bowels. In navy boot camp when we'd marched to the dispensary and were lined up for our blood draws, I grew so anxious that I actually passed out waiting in line. They gave me smelling salts and put me back in line. By the time they drew my blood, I barely flinched. All of my adrenaline had been spent.

Darlene was explaining. "At first, Belle didn't want me involved at all. She was going to crash her car into a wall or something. But suicide would affect her life insurance policy and . . ." Darlene's gaze went to the kitchen.

I followed her eyes and saw Trevor enter through the side door. He wore Dockers and a black T-shirt that showed off his gym pecs. He entered the living room and placed a roll of duct tape on the coffee table. Darlene whispered in his ear.

"Well, now that we're all here . . . Who thought of the snakes?" I asked with a bravado I hoped was convincing.

Trevor spoke up. "That was my idea. Belle and Darlene were my neighbors when Belle was stationed in Pensacola." His eyes looked teary. "Belle treated me better than my own mother did."

"That coffee smells good. Mind if I pour myself a cup?" I started toward the kitchen. Hot coffee could make a good projectile, enough of a distraction for me to get the hell out of there.

"Sorry, Tess, but I don't think so." Darlene spoke the words, but Trevor's body blocked the entrance into the kitchen. "Trev, pull the living room curtains closed, will you?"

Uh, oh. Not an encouraging sign.

Trevor picked up where he'd left off. "When I was just a kid, Wade Matthews did this to my face." His hand brushed the scar.

I shivered, whether from chill or fright, I wasn't sure.

Darlene took up the story. "Trev moved here only a few years after we did. One summer the three of us were having dinner at the Spaghetti Factory downtown. We spotted Matthews at a nearby table. Later, we looked him up in the phone book and found his home in Borrego. When Belle planned her euthanasia, Trev suggested we throw suspicion on Matthews."

Trevor approached. "By then we'd learned about the rape charge against him. He should've gone to prison for that, so not only was there revenge for me, there was justice for the rape victim, too. From talking to Belle, I knew Darlene had been raised in the Church of God with Signs Following. Matthews was the perfect fall guy; at least that's how Belle and I saw it."

Darlene was pacing again, back and forth between the coffee table and the chairs. It seemed in my best interest to keep her talking. "So the idea was to perform the euthanasia with a snake, to throw suspicion on Matthews?"

"Would've worked, too, if you hadn't interfered," Darlene asserted. "Every time we thought things were going well, you mucked up the works."

"I'm not the one who put Matthews in his dentist's chair the day of the murder," I objected.

They looked chagrined. Trevor admitted, "The dentist appointment threw us. But then I got the idea of offering psychic help to the police, to point them back in Matthews's direction. I thought we might convince the cops that the dentist was mistaken, especially if we went through you, since you were friends with Sergeant Dixon."

I meandered a foot or two closer to the front door. The sky did not fall in. "How come the cops never found anything linking you two? They tracked phone records back three months from the time of the murder and couldn't find squat."

Darlene stood directly across from me, about two feet away. "Once Belle hatched her plan, we were very discreet about our meetings. We stopped calling Trev. We created new e-mail accounts, and replaced our hard drives right after Belle died."

If I didn't stop hyperventilating, I was going to pass out. I tried to focus. I felt like an arachnophobe staring at a two-foot tarantula. Breathe in; breathe out. Breathing is so simple—done well without the slightest thought—when the object of a phobia isn't hovering. Maybe if I took my eyes off the needle. I turned toward Trevor. "How did you pull off that psychic test at the police station?"

He shrugged. "I can't explain it scientifically, but I really do have a gift."

"Is that how you knew about my black boots the first time you called? You hadn't planted the bug in my house then."

Darlene offered something that might have been a laugh under different circumstances. "Remember the day you visited me in the hospital?"

I nodded.

"You played right into our hands. You left your purse on my nightstand when you went to get a vase for the flowers. I wrote down your credit card and driver's license numbers while you were gone. Later, I was able to get your last five credit card purchases. I e-mailed Trev from a public library, and told him you'd just bought something from Boot World that had silver trim. He took it from there."

I moved another few inches toward the front door. I tried to do it subtly, but at size 16, subtlety in movement is a challenge. Less fat in my diet, more support of Free Trade products, and environmentally appropriate disposal of household batteries were among my silent offers to the Goddess if only she'd rid the planet of hypodermics immediately. "Did Belle know when it would happen?"

"Generally, yes, but she didn't want to know the exact moment. I chose the deadliest snake I could find in the research lab. I wanted it to be quick; I didn't want her to suffer." With one hand, she wiped tears away, but the needle remained firmly in the other hand's grip. "We made love that morning. When she dozed off, I got the snake from the garage where I'd hidden it, and . . ." Darlene looked at me with such sadness that sympathy almost overwhelmed my terror. "Afterwards . . . when it was over . . . I bathed and dressed her. Trev came over to help me move her body. We picked the UCSD Snake Path because that's where Matthews raped that girl."

"Why all the hair and buttons?"

"Belle realized Matthews might have an alibi for whatever time I picked for her death. She wanted to make sure the police could find an alternative theory, without looking in my direction. So, we tried to make the crime scene look like the work of a psycho concerned about trace evidence."

The needle now loomed bigger than a Jesuit's vocabulary; as huge as Mick Jagger's ego. Nothing else in the whirling, spinning room mattered.

Darlene reduced the distance between us by a foot.

I focused as hard as I could and came up with a plan: I'd toss the sewing basket at her and dash for the front door. I wasn't really worried about Trevor—he seemed to take his cues from Darlene. My muscles tensed as I prepared for action. "If you kill me with that, all of Belle's efforts to keep you out of trouble will be down the drain. She didn't want you to spend the rest of your life in prison."

"Don't be such a drama queen. Nembutal won't kill you; it'll just buy me time." She gave a slight nod. Before I could brace for it, Trevor moved behind me, forced me into an armchair, and sealed a strip of duct tape across my mouth.

Darlene placed the needle on the TV stand. For a moment, I thought I'd somehow managed a reprieve. But then she pulled a rubber tourniquet from her pocket. Trevor held my arm in place while she constricted my upper arm with the band. Her fingers probed the vessels on the inside of my elbow. She reached for the needle, tapped its cylinder, and pressed the hypodermic plunger a notch. A drop of clear fluid emerged.

My lungs felt like Mount St. Helens. I tried to break Trevor's hold but I felt my knees buckle. The last thing I remember was the smell of astringent. Boot camp, take two.

36

DOWN THE HATCH

"When you forced that freshly milked rattler to bite you, you said it would throw off any suspicion the police had about you. How did Tess see through that? How could things go this wrong?" Trevor gripped Tess's upper torso while Darlene carried her feet. They slid her into the rear of her Infiniti, which they'd moved to Darlene's garage.

"You got her cell phone, right?" Darlene asked.

Trevor nodded.

"Well, then it's 'down the hatch'!" Darlene joked.

No response.

"The hatch, get it? It's a hatchback? Oh, look, it's not so awful, Trev. Don't worry about me. Malaysia's got no extradition treaty with the U.S. They need nurses. It's been a while, but they're still dealing with the aftermath of the tsunami. I managed to book that flight for Kuala Lumpur out of L.A. tonight. They had other seats available. Sure you won't change your mind and go with?"

Trevor smiled and shook his head no. *"It's just as easy for me to disappear in New York. Besides, I already know the language." Trevor's demeanor shifted. "Darlene, you're going to make it. I know this."*

"Thanks, Trev. You'll do OK, too. You're only an accessory to euthanasia. They won't bust their chops to find you." Darlene handed Trevor Tess's car keys. "You drive her car. I'll follow you in mine."

Fifteen minutes later, they stood in the farthest corner of the deserted top level of the parking garage at the hospital where Darlene worked. Trevor handed Darlene the Infiniti's keys. "What now?"

Darlene pulled a wad of cash from her wallet and pressed it into Trevor's hand. "Now is the perfect time for you to adopt a 'Don't Ask/Don't Tell' policy. Take a cab home, pack up, and get out of San Diego as quick as you can."

Trevor stood numbly.

Darlene hurried him. "Get out of here now! Go!" She gave him a motherly hug, and turned away. She glimpsed the peachy unscarred side of his face as he walked toward the exit and out into the night.

Darlene looked at her watch. 7:45 P.M.. That last dose of Nembutal would wear off shortly. She locked the Infiniti and headed into the building. A few minutes later she re-emerged, carrying a cardboard box. Fumes from car exhaust had given her a headache, but the headache was the least of her worries. She had a connecting flight from San Diego to LAX in two hours and needed to get to Lindbergh Field, pronto.

Darlene placed the box on the concrete floor and spoke softly into the vacant gray parking garage. "I can't stay here, shooting her with Nembutal," she whispered. "And if she wakes up soon and gets help, the authorities could be waiting for me at LAX. Damn, I hate this! This is not how I wanted things to go! Oh, Belle! How did you convince yourself this would all go smoothly? Wishful thinking, wishful thinking. The whole plan was probably just a giant distraction from your diagnosis. But, honey, I don't really blame you. I blame this meddling woman!"

She looked around. This level of the parking garage was still deserted. She unlocked and lifted the Infiniti's hatch. When she opened the cardboard box, a dank scent burst from it. She looked at the reptile's terra cotta scales, interspersed with ecru in an intricate mosaic. It seemed both beautiful and timid. She closed her eyes and breathed deeply. Humming a hymn, Darlene reached into the box and grasped the snake, laid it next to Tess in the trunk, and locked the hatch door. She tried not to appear too hurried as she headed for her car.

37

WOMB WITH NO VIEW

I woke up in the fetal position, in a womb with no view. Everything hurt: My head, joints, back, neck, and legs ached with pain, and my abdominal incision throbbed and burned. One hand tingled with numbness. I lay on my side, and my shoulder screamed from bearing my weight too long. I lifted myself up a fraction of an inch and eased my shoulder joint.

My eyes stung. I couldn't see. Had I been blinded or was it simply the lack of light?

The ammonia smell of urine permeated the tight tenebrous space, joining a ghoul's potpourri of exhaust fumes and something musky. The bristly surface where I lay scratched my skin. I shivered. My mouth told me I'd been sucking phlegm lollipops dipped in dirt. I strained to breathe.

Where the hell was I? Thoughts swam upstream against residual Nembutal and nausea. Finally I remembered. Darlene. The needle. What did she inject me with? Embalming fluid?

My stinging eyes began to adjust to the darkness. Near my face, I saw a bulbous lump. I looped in and out of consciousness for a while before I recognized it as a wheel well. I was in a car trunk. I looked longer and harder. I was lying diagonally on my left side in the Silver Bullet's hatch, facing the rear seat.

I sensed something, and lay still, waiting for more. Nothing. Just my imagination.

If I was already dead and my current status reflected the afterlife, I really, really should've read those *Watchtowers*. If, contrary to most indicators, I was still alive, there was hope. The rear doors on either side of the Silver Bullet had pulls to unlock the hatch. All I had to do was fend off nausea, disorientation, and fumes long enough to reach over the rear seat. No biggie.

Suddenly my right calf muscle clenched in a severe charley horse. I stretched my leg to ease the cramp, and heard something like the popped effervescence of a Lilliputian Coke can.

I lay there gathering strength, trying to clear my head, and felt something move down near my feet. This time, I knew it wasn't my imagination. I tried to recall what I might have in the trunk—something cylindrical that might roll toward me? Couldn't remember traveling with any rolling pins lately. I felt a slight pressure against my lower leg, like a lover's foot brushing gently against mine under the covers. I tried desperately to make sense of all this, but my brain displayed a Windows hourglass, the way the operating system does when it has trouble processing. More oxygen might help. I took a deep breath, and with it came a hit of funky odor.

Suddenly I knew. Oh. My. God. How *could* you, Darlene? Part of me wanted to laugh from the exquisite tension. And a big part of me wanted to reboot the brain that concluded a snake was in the trunk with me. But the hourglass had disappeared. Neural circuits zoomed, flushed by a radical jolt of adrenaline.

I needed something that eludes certain commanders-in-chief: an exit strategy. I remembered learning somewhere that snakes can't hear. I could scream. Maybe someone would hear me and come to the rescue. For all I knew, the Silver Bullet might be fifty miles from the nearest human, but it was worth a try.

In preparation for a hearty yell, I took a deep breath, which triggered bronchial hacking. I struggled not to jostle the snake. After a few puny attempts, I managed one decent scream. I tensed, waiting for the snake to bite, but nothing happened. Snakes really can't hear. But apparently, neither did anyone else. No response.

I concentrated and tried not to puke. This had not been a fun day. In fact, the past few months hadn't been the kindest. A rattler under my bed, a mutant raccoon, breast cancer, a mastectomy, a deviant scarecrow, and now, me and a beastie, locked together in a car trunk! This is not Mother Teresa-type karma. I had definitely not kissed the right butt in some prior existence.

What could I do besides scream? What did I have available to me? I could feel netting from the trunk organizer, somewhere around my knees. Something small and metallic, perhaps a seat belt anchor, was near my left arm. What else was at my disposal? Enough oxygen for a little while longer.

Of course, I also possessed internal tools: intellect, will, faith. Yes, faith. That's what Darlene used to handle snakes. Maybe the One who spared me from cancer would allow me to grasp the snake safely, if I tried with enough conviction.

As I reached tentatively behind me, I had a religious epiphany: I may not be a Jersey Jew-Girl, but I'm not a member of the Church of God with Signs Following either.

I brought my hand back slowly to the trunk floor, and began exploring the hard metal object near my arm. The snake didn't react. I fumbled with the object and recognized it—my fishing knife! The one I'd accidentally left in my car when Darlene and I went to the O.B. pier.

Now I had a weapon, but the snake was behind me. To kill it, I'd have to stab it square in the head. Now that I was more able to focus, I could feel its presence along my side. I tried to discern the snake's exact position. The tail felt close to my feet. I sensed the snake's light pressure all the way to my tailbone. That had to be where the head was. But were the tingles traveling my spine triggered by my terror or by contact with the snake?

If I jabbed behind me at a snake I couldn't see, and missed, I might lacerate my own spinal cord. But if I didn't do something soon, I'd suffocate or eventually die of snakebite. Some situations are worth a stab in the dark.

I took one deep breath that scalded my lungs, reached behind me, and thrust. A lancinating bite on my hip registered nanoseconds before the knife hit its mark. The snake thrashed briefly, and then lay still.

Now what? Who knew what kind of slinky, scaly companion had been spooning me? If an *Oxyuranus microlepidotus*, I wouldn't live long enough to learn how to pronounce my killer's name correctly.

Survival optimism kicked in. I'd watched enough nature shows to realize snakes don't inject venom every time they bite. Maybe this snake was saving its venom for a mouse with mayo, hold the Camillo. Maybe it wasn't even a poisonous snake; maybe Darlene was just trying to intimidate me.

I rolled over. It felt glorious to move again! Jerkily, I lowered the Silver Bullet's rear seat and pulled the hatch opener on the rear door. When I popped the trunk and fresh air hit me, my heart burst into paeans of gratitude.

My body had never felt so utterly shitty before in my entire life. (Well, *maybe* that ouzo hangover on my twenty-fourth birthday.) A peculiar metallic taste now competed with phlegm, fumes, and dust for primacy in my taste buds. If the snake had injected venom, I had precious little time. Judging from the increasing pain in my hip, I was pretty sure it had.

I climbed out and got my bearings. I was in a parking structure. There was an elevator along one wall. I grabbed my trunk companion, knowing if I could make it to a hospital, they'd want to know what bit me.

About a dozen yards from the elevator, I collapsed. Weird tingling traveled through my legs and arms—the snake's venom must contain a neurotoxin. I felt as weak as five gallons of tea brewed with one bag. I was radically thirsty, irritable, bleeding, in pain, and had likely peed my pants. Good thing I'm from Jersey, or I might have been discouraged.

My legs were rapidly growing numb. My arms had more mobility, so I dragged myself along on my elbows. When I reached the elevator, it took all I had left to push the call button.

I'm a bit fuzzy on how I made it from the elevator to the ER, but suspect folks waiting for the elevator expedited matters when they saw a half-paralyzed woman and a dead snake on the elevator floor.

Everything in the ER moved too slowly until I was seen by a doctor, and too fast once care had arrived. I must have moved in and out of consciousness, because I don't even recall them starting an IV. People and conversations blipped like video game characters all around me, yet at the same time, seemed somehow distant.

"Respirator!"

"Who's got the snake?"

"Page Dr. Harley, STAT!"

"Southern Pacific rattler; injected about 120 cc of venom."

"These are recent mastectomy and reconstruction scars. Do we know if her immune system's been compromised by chemo?"

"Morphine sulfate, 20 milligrams, STAT, and start the antivenin."

"Did you know rock ground squirrels have a chemical in their blood that protects them from rattlesnake venom? I saw it on Animal Planet."

"Uncrimp that tubing, will you?"

I sank into blissful sleep that felt as close to Mother Teresa karma as I'm ever likely to get.

38

TROUBADOURS ARE DANCING

The week between Christmas and New Year's is culturally post-coital: a peculiar sloshing together of relief, happiness, exhaustion, satisfaction, occasional regret, peace, and antici-pation.

With two days left in the year, I worked my way through a hearty gym routine, then kept an appointment with Dr. Min Fan, my Chinese medicine specialist. He looks like Bud-dha with a Bowflex. Being in his presence is as soothing as a bubble bath. To me, everything about this healer conveys peace, except his needles. I'd made it abundantly clear at a previous appointment that I wasn't interested in acupuncture because sharp pointed objects were involved. We'd settled on a regimen of herbs to strengthen my immune system.

I took the prescription he gave me today, written entirely in Chinese characters, which probably said, "Patient's a real pip," and filled it at a fusty herb store in Linda Vista. A final stop at Fashion Valley mall to exchange a gift and pick up my new cell phone completed my errands. I don't know what happened to my old cell; the cops never found it at Darlene's or Trevor's.

Back home, I was trying to figure out the phone's functionalities without reading the user's manual, when Lana returned from a Reiki class at San Diego Hospice.

"Check out my new cell phone," I urged. "It's got a built-in camera, calculator, currency converter, backscratcher, and tea strainer."

Her mesmerizing eyes crinkled in a smile. "You sure about the backscratcher?" Her gaze landed on the coffee table. "Oh! Tess, remember the day you found the scarecrow in the backyard?"

"How could I forget?"

"You heard someone's cell phone ring, but you could never figure out whose phone it was?"

"Must've been a neighbor's," I muttered.

Lana picked up a *National Geographic* from our coffee table, turned to a page with the corner crimped, and read aloud, "If you hear a cell phone ring outdoors, you may be startled to learn the caller is a starling. Starlings are fabulous mimics. Observers note they've added the warbling of cell phones to their repertoire." She handed me the magazine.

I recalled a starling proudly sitting on one of the scarecrow's outstretched arms. I'll be darned. One more piece of the puzzle.

Lana chatted with me in the kitchen as I prepared a broccoli cheese quiche for dinner. She grated Muenster and cheddar and shared poignant moments from her Reiki class, as I beat eggs, chopped broccoli, sliced mushrooms, and sprinkled seasonings. Though Nate was currently in Argentina, Lana was smiling a lot these days. I think she was happy I was still around.

While the quiche baked, we walked the dogs, stopping to socialize with our rap-loving neighbor, Smacker. We then settled in for dinner. Such normal domesticity felt wonderful to me after the weirdness of recent events. We sat on the couch watching TV, ridding our teeth of broccoli bits, and wishing one of us had thought about dessert. A program in which a math genius uses his skills to help his FBI agent sibling solve crimes captured our attention.

"I like this show," I told Lana. "If this dude could help the FBI, it makes me wonder . . . well, I'm a math major. I loved the adrenaline rush of trying to find Belle's killer. Do you think maybe someday, there'll be another 'case' I can work on? Another mystery in my life? Another venture to be followed?"

She gathered our dishes, loaded them into the dishwasher, and returned. I thought she hadn't heard me, and was about to repeat the question when she answered, "Remember what I told you about the conjunctions of Neptune and Pluto in your Eighth House? You'll inevitably be drawn to mystery, life, and death, Tess." She tousled my hair lightly. "Silly girl, the troubadours are dancing for you! Fairies are watching over you! A new year is ready to launch; a new tale is already in motion!"

She hugged me good night and headed to bed.

In my own room, I smiled to myself as I undressed, wondering what on earth dancing troubadours had to do with my future as an amateur sleuth, if, indeed, I had one. If my future as a snoop was up for grabs, so was my romantic future. Lee Anne had called to say she'd met someone else. Would I meet someone who would want what my post-breast cancer physique could offer?

I looked in the mirror and examined the thick but strong body reflected there. My abdominal incision was losing its sore, reddish hue, fading to a pale purple. The thin scar bisecting the left breast mound had healed well. Three distinct circular scars the size of cigarette burns near the top of my pubic hairline reminded me of the drain tubes I'd had to contend with. Much rather see the scars than wear those friggin' drains. The snakebite wound was already little more than a memory. My hair and skin looked good, and hale muscle tone rewarded my recently intensified gym workouts. I'd asked much of my body lately, but it had graciously lived up to my demands.

I donned my pj's and climbed on the bed. Raj sat at my feet, wanting connection. At my current stage of spiritual evolution, I believe the best companion for the road of life is a dog. God probably comes next, then friends, family, Jesus, Buddha, and Groucho Marx. "Raj, when I was a kid and Grandma Camillo took me to church, the preacher would tell us to 'stand and sing the doxology.' For the longest time, I thought it was the dogs-ology."

Raj liked that one. His tail ticktocked with joy.

"You never judge anyone by race, looks, social status, or income. You love me unconditionally. You're the most god-like being I know, and sometimes that scares me."

Raj kissed my hand.

I quickly added, "Other times it delights me."

He barked softly three times.

"Yes, I know 'God' and 'dog' have the same three letters."

Raj approved of my translation with a warm lick. I crawled under the covers, and continued petting his familiar, comforting coat.

"You have a sense of humor, right, Raj? God has one, too, I'm sure, and it favors the ironic. I mean, linear-brained lesbian math majors fall in love with right-brained straight Tai Chi instructors. Belle asked something of Darlene that seemed utterly self*less*, yet was impossibly self*ish*. I managed to solve a murder, only to realize the victim pleaded for her own death."

I sighed and looked out the sliding door at the night sky. If I hadn't left that slider open one day last August, the rattlesnake wouldn't have slipped inside my room. I was about to conjecture further 'what if's' when I shifted positions and realized Raj had fallen asleep. He's better at chasing balls and juicy kisses than philosophizing, confirmation of his divine nature.

The author found the following resources very helpful:

Choices in Healing: Integrating the Best of Conventional and Complementary Approaches to Cancer, by Michael Lerner. ISBN: 0262621045.
Speak the Language of Healing: Living with Breast Cancer without Going to War, by Susan Kuner et al. ISBN: 1573241687.
http://www.susanloveMD.org
http://www.breastcancer.org